# REDRUM

FIDA
1st edition
(First German edition)
Copyright © 2018
(First American edition)
Copyright © 2019
REDRUM BOOKS, Berlin
Publisher: Michael Merhi
Translated by Simon Kossov
Editor (American edition): Jasmin Kraft
Cover design and concept:
MIMO GRAPHICS by using an
illustration by Shutterstock.

ISBN 978-3-95957-563-8

E-Mail: merhi@gmx.net
www.redrum-verlag.de

YouTube: Michael Merhi Books
Facebook: REDRUM BOOKS
Facebook Group:
REDRUM BOOKS—Nichts für Pussys!

# Stefanie Maucher

# FIDA

**The Book:**

What would you do if your child just disappeared? If you don't know if it's still alive or dead? Would your family grow closer together or break under the load?

At what point would you give up hope? And how far would you go if you found the culprit?

Thirteen-year-old Laura didn't come home after visiting the library. The police quickly found a suspect – but no trace of the girl. Tatjana has been searching for her daughter for more than a year and isn't willing to give up hope …

Tom always wanted a pet. Preferably a puppy that obeys his commands. But at that time his father already knew about Tom's vicious, sadistic drives and so the wish for a toy remained unfulfilled for a long time. To this day! Because Tom is grown up now and he thinks it's time to fulfill his wishes by himself. Time for Fida!

Vincent Prize 2013 awarded in the category of 'Best German Novel'.

**The Author:**

Hard, suspenseful and often far too realistic ... Stefanie Maucher's stories crawl under her readers' skin. Born in Stuttgart in 1976, the author loves to take a look into the deepest and darkest human abysses and relentlessly talk about what she finds there.
The mother of two now lives in Eastern Germany, where she works as a proofreader and translator whenever she's not writing her own books.

# Stefanie Maucher

# FIDA

Thriller

# April 10, 2017

She quickly crosses the street and hurries along the sidewalk with her head down. Past the crumbling walls of an old residential house, from which the plaster peels off in large chunks, and with a fallow meadow adjacent to it. The wind from behind presses the gray coat against her legs. It blows the jingling *Ping!* of a bicycle bell to her ears just a second before she manages to avoid a cyclist who swears while he overtakes her and splashes the dirty water of a puddle on her.

She stumbles and almost gets stuck on a bush that lines the wayside. Nettles protrude between the bare, thorny branches of the dead shrub, in which wire, string and other rubbish have become entangled, and only scantily hide the wasteland behind them. Right next to the dilapidated house, an old rotary clothes dryer with torn strings rusts away. Further back on the abandoned site, rotten planks are insufficiently covering an old, probably long dried out well shaft, with not much left of its brick border. Almost as if the owner of this ruin wanted someone to break his neck sooner or later while roaming his property.

She doesn't like this scruffy part of the way, so she usually accelerates her steps here. The dilapidated property reminds her too much of her own wasteland, which she carries around with her … of the emptiness she feels since she began to walk this path regularly.

Only sometimes she walks slower, wondering what this house might have to tell. Then she makes up stories about it, with which she tries to distract herself from the dark thoughts that accompany her all the time. Maybe people who loved each other very much once lived there. They were happy together until old age, although they couldn't have children. On Saturdays the man washed his car, polished the car paint until it shone spotlessly, while his wife hung up the laundry – in the garden that she lovingly cared for. Maybe a neighbor boy was getting paid to mow the lawn.

Now the house is empty. Nobody enters it anymore. But if you'd go inside, you could still find the testimonies of a fulfilled life there. Possibly the man worked in the now-empty factory across the street. When she and her own husband moved to this area, more than a decade ago, the factory was still in use, but nothing is produced here today. This building is also dilapidating. Graffiti decorates the once red brick walls, the windows are dirty, opaque or already smashed.

"Asshole!" the woman in her coat screams after the cyclist while she's still struggling not to lose her balance. Her right heel gets caught in the wire that protrudes from the bushes like a primitive tripping hazard. She bends over. A stabbing pain shoots through her ankle, but she manages not to fall down. Only what she carries with her slips out of her hand and falls to the ground. Tears shoot into her eyes, but she vigorously blinks them away while she's caught in a wave of anger. On the cyclist and on the city that doesn't want to spend money on a cycle path. On the dirt in the bushes, for whose maintenance nobody feels responsible.

The cyclist turns to her. Maybe it was her insult that made him aware of his ruthlessness. He brakes and turns. Tatjana has caught her breath again, puts her hands on her hips and stares angrily at him. She expects him to turn around and come back to apologize to her. Instead, he drives past her, turns, and—she can hardly

12

believe so much impudence and wickedness—then deliberately speeds through the puddle again.

With a smug grin on his lips he shouts: "It's just a bit
of water!" before he pedals hard and quickly cycles
away.

"You son of a bitch!" she yells at him with outrage. If
his bike had a license plate, she'd go straight to the police. The paint is striking: an orange-red flame pattern on
a black background, but she doubts that the police
would look for the bike, find the guy and punish him for
his insolence. Even though the cyclist is almost out of
sight, she adds another shot and yells: "You asshole!"

It's undetermined anger at everything that she gives
free rein to with this outcry. For the moment, it covers
up her other emotions and it distracts her from the
morbid thoughts that are invading Tatjana's consciousness on this abandoned part of her way. The anger also
prevents her from sitting on the side of the street and
bursting into tears.

There's something furious and upright about her at
this moment of anger, but just a moment later her narrow shoulders sag again and she seems as abandoned as
the place itself. As if she belonged here. With her gray
coat and the fringy hair that hasn't seen a hairdresser for
months and flutters powerlessly in the wind. Just as lost
as the leaves lying on the ground, or the frayed cord
hanging in the thicket, colored by the street dirt and the
exhaust fumes.

She hastily collects her fallen sheet protectors and
wipes off the drops of splash water that have landed on
them. Then she presses them to her chest like a treasure.
Slowly, now slightly limping, she walks on. She looks
older than she is. If she would tone her hair and dress
differently and put on a smile, one couldn't help but

describing her as an attractive woman. But during the last year she's aged by decades. Especially inwardly. Her worries and the agonizing uncertainty have left marks on her face; wrinkles have dug into her forehead and the sides of her lips, which are now mostly squeezed together. Above all, however, they've left scars on her soul. They rob her of sleep, which is also visible on her. Her skin is pale, with dark shadows under her eyes, and if Edvard Munch were to paint her, the resulting painting might be called 'Before the Scream'.

Once a week she walks along here, with bulged coat pockets and tired steps, always following the same route. It starts at her home, takes her past the first bus stop, then to a playground, which is a popular meeting place for mothers with small children in the afternoon. A few streets further on there's a bakery and a small kiosk. She makes a short stop at each of these places to leave something behind. Then she turns into the long street which leads her past this abandoned place, where she just stumbled, to the next bus stop. Avoiding the desolation would be a detour. Whether it's storming, snowing or the sun is shining: she walks this route every Wednesday. Sometimes she's on the verge of not going. Simply sitting at home and following the advice of her husband, who has been shaking his head over her for a long time and doesn't understand why she keeps doing this to herself.

"Tatjana, why do you torture yourself so badly?" he's asked her many times. Jochen doesn't understand that she cannot do otherwise. She has to walk the route, even if it seems senseless to him. He says that she's only driving herself crazy with it. She has to learn to get to terms with it, as difficult as it may be. Sometimes she thinks he's right, envies him for how he deals with it all. She's

14

aware that it's anything but easy for him as well, but on the outside it looks as if it hardly bothers him. In other moments she almost hates him for just being able to go on, day after day, trying to lead his damn life as if nothing elemental were missing.

But nothing is normal anymore, nothing at all! At the beginning he'd accompany her, then he stopped and meanwhile Jochen openly criticizes that she can't finally let go of it.

"Why do you tear this wound open again and again?" he asked her with a reproachful tone during the last argument. Since then she has given up discussing with him. It would seem like a betrayal to her not to go anymore. It would be a surrender and an admission she's not willing to make. If she's ever to find peace again, if she finally wants to sleep peacefully again, then she mustn't bury her last spark of hope. Not before she's found what she's looking for – or at least finds something to mourn and bury.

*You mustn't give up*, she keeps telling herself before she leaves for her weekly walk. *Nothing in the world disappears without a trace.*

Finally she reaches the roofed bus stop at the end of the street. A glance at her wristwatch tells her that due to her little accident it had taken her longer than usual to get there. She looks around. The bus is already in sight. A small dot at the end of the seemingly endless road she had just walked along. She usually has a few minutes before it arrives and she gets on. She only drives a few stops to the city park with its mighty old oaks, where many people go for walks every day.

Now she has to hurry. Her nervous fingers reach into her dented coat pocket, in which a handful of nails are gently jingling. The hammer is in the other pocket. She'll

15

need it later when she's in the park. Although sticking posters is prohibited here, she hastily uses the duct tape to attach one of her transparent sleeves to the glass pane. She's barely done when she hears the droning of the bus, which stops next to her with unpleasantly squeaking brakes. The doors open with a hissing noise. Her gaze lovingly grazes her daughter's face before she enters. How beautifully Laura's hair shone on the day this picture was taken. She wore her favorite sweatshirt, her fingers played with the cord of her hood and she smiled happily into the camera. 'MISSING' is written in large letters above the photo.

# March 6, 2016

Amused, Oliver Nagel, the branch manager of a drugstore in the city, noticed that a horde of giggling girls stormed into his shop. They purposefully headed for the cosmetics, where they spent a few minutes testing powders, lipsticks and nail polishes before laughing and spraying each other with perfume samples. His colleague standing next to him sourly distorted the corners of her mouth and was about to intervene, but he put a hand on her arm to appease her.

"Leave the girls alone, Mrs. Weber. These are our customers of tomorrow."

With a lenient smile, he watched as one of the girls left the crowd of her friends and approached the vending machine that the market offered for ordering and printing pictures, while the others continued to try out the range of cosmetics. The girl at the vending machine was slightly taller than her friends and looked like a young tree to him. Slim and tall. In contrast to the others, whose faces were decorated with a kind of war paint, she looked very natural. She still abstained from make-up. Her long dark hair was braided into a thick plait that fell over her shoulder. Concentrated, she frowned as she followed the instructions of the machine.

Nagel was busy in a side corridor within earshot when a friend joined her, looked over her shoulder and asked, "Laura, how long will it take you? We want to go on." He overheard Laura complaining that the format she wanted wasn't immediately available and that she had to order the prints first.

"Hopefully the pictures will arrive in time," she continued. "Otherwise, I won't have a birthday present for my mother."

"What are you giving her?" the bored-looking girlfriend asked, more dutiful than interested. Nevertheless, Laura excessively told her that she had scanned old pictures in the last few days and had copied them to a memory card. Pictures of herself as a baby, of the first day at school, but she had also made several new ones that her mother didn't know yet. She'd also digitized the few pictures that her mother still had from her own childhood. Photos that also showed the grandparents she'd never really met because they died when Laura was very young. At a flea market she had found a worn, nostalgic photo album that looked as old as the antique books her mother had inherited and treasured. They took a place of honor on the shelf in her favorite room – a small reading chamber she had set up. A small wood-burning stove provided this room with pleasant warmth in winter, a comfortable wingchair stood in it, and when she was still little, she had often sat on her sheepskin at her feet and listened to her mother reading from her books. By using an image editing program, she had refreshed the old photographs, which were slowly losing their gloss and color, and she wanted to give her mother a special treat by giving her the pictures in this old leather-bound album, whose corners were reinforced and decorated with wonderfully crafted brass fittings – as a present for her fortieth birthday.

Laura told all this to the girl with the bored look who listened with only half her ear and devoted most of her attention to the false eyelashes on the shelf next to her while she selected her pictures. Branch manager Nagel smiled. A few days ago his girlfriend had told him that she was expecting a child. He had never thought about what it was like to be a father before, but since he knew about the pregnancy, he looked differently at children and teenagers. The nagging children in the cashier's area almost made him shiver in panic, but when he saw girls like this one, the thought of offspring didn't seem so frightening anymore. On the other hand, her bored friend with her big earrings, the nose piercing and the gaudy make-up served his horror of a bitchy teenage daughter.

When the order was finally placed, the machine calmed Laura's scheduling concerns by informing her that her order would be ready for pickup at the store within three to five days.

"Okay, that should do it. They'll be here by Friday at the latest", she commented on the information.

"Come on now, Laura!" her friend demanded with an annoyed tone of voice. "The others are waiting."

Oliver Nagel watched, completely absorbed in his own thoughts, as the girls—pulling a cloud of noble scents behind them—went off towards the exit.

\*\*\*

Ordering the pictures had taken longer than Laura had thought and Kerstin was urging. Normally she wore her 'memory heart' on a little chain around her neck, but now Laura carelessly stuffed her USB stick, which was hidden in a heart-shaped pendant, into the stupid bag she felt too old for. It was a gift from her mother that she was terribly angry about at that moment. At the age of twelve she thought the bag was cool, but now she was thirteen and found it embarrassing to have to go to school day after day with this children's bag. She'd been annoying her parents for a few weeks now because she wanted a new one, but her mother said that 120 euros were overpriced for the model she wanted. But the old bag already had a hole, even if she had drilled it herself to put forward one more point for the desired new purchase. A hole through which her chic storage medium fell unnoticed in order to be pushed under a shelf by the next pair of passing shoes.

After visiting the drug store, her friends wanted to go to the ice cream parlor. It was to be a first joint visit, as the parlor closed every autumn and reopened in spring. But Laura's best friend had other plans.

"Come on, Laura!" Kerstin grouched. "Let's go to the park. I don't feel like ice cream at all."

Laura immediately figured out her intentions. Kerstin wanted to go to the city park, where the boys from her school often loitered in the afternoons. She openly raved about Patrick, a boy from the parallel class, despite the fact that he had only been dating Jenny for a few weeks, with whom they were also friends. It was an explosive situation between the girlfriends who slowly became rivals.

If you asked Laura, she wasn't in love with anyone. She seemed shy, sometimes a bit insecure, so it didn't matter how nervous she got when Tobi, Patrick's best friend, was around her. She used her friend's obvious infatuation as a welcome distraction from herself as soon as the subject came to boys. Just a year ago she had found boys generally terribly stupid – she still did. Most of them were idiots. Except for Tobi, with whom she hardly spoke a word, but who nevertheless seemed profound, interesting and somehow a kindred spirit.

Although she actually wanted ice cream, Laura let herself be persuaded by Kerstin and accompanied her to the park. Patrick wasn't there, but Tobi was. It didn't take long for Kerstin to spot him. Now Laura watched jealously as Kerstin threw herself at Tobi, coquettishly jingling her eyelashes as she herself felt like the fifth wheel and stepped back and forth insecurely. It wasn't the first time Laura was annoyed at how confident her friend was with him, while she just stood there stupidly and couldn't say a word. And Tobi also seemed to like it. He didn't appreciate her look, hung on Kerstin's every word, while she obviously interrogated him about Patrick. The two had apparently completely forgotten Laura and concentrated fully on gathering information and passing it on. So she had all the time in the world to become aware of the pimples on her forehead. Time to find her own eyelashes far too short and to fervently hate her mother for a moment for forbidding Laura to use make-up before her next birthday.

"Your father wouldn't like it – and neither do I!" she always said. "We can talk about it again when you're fourteen."

So Laura would have to wait three endless months. Kerstin's mother wasn't so stuffy. She'd even allowed her to get a nose piercing and a second hole for earrings. No surprise that Kerstin was much cooler.

Then the most terrible thing she could imagine at that moment happened. Patrick approached the small group.

"Hello, Kitty!" he roared loudly, which made the young ones around him turn their gazes to him. "What are you doing here, sweetcheeks?" he added provocatively, while he rudely bumped into them. "Why don't you play in the sandbox with your Barbies?"

Now all eyes turned to Laura. Also Tobi's. Laura opened her mouth, wanted to give a snappy reply and saw Tobi grinning broadly and expectantly. The blood shot into her cheeks, which were now glowing, and instead of the devastating verbal blow only a stammering caw came out of her mouth.

"Uhm, uhm, uhm." Patrick mimicked her while Tobi laughed. Even Kerstin started giggling. Tears came to Laura's eyes. "You're such a piece of shit," she hissed. It was all so embarrassing! Before anyone could see that she was crying like a baby, she turned around and ran away.

"Laura, wait!" Kerstin called after her, but Laura just wanted to leave. Laura ran a good part of the way that she usually drove back by bus until she ran out of breath.

Running had done her good. Every step that led her away from the park and the mean laughter ... but now she felt a painful burning and stinging in her side. Laura slowed down her pace. Sniffing, she oriented herself and realized that she wasn't far away from the city library. She rummaged in her pocket for her wallet. Yes, she had her identity card with her. Very good. There was also a bus stop at the library. She could take the bus home from there later.

Laura's mood got better when she entered the library where she wanted to spend the next few hours. Not very much, but enough to keep her from letting show.

"Hello, Mrs. Stemmler," she greeted the librarian with a smile. She was about to put a pile of books back on the shelves. Mrs. Stemmler was always nice and had a good tip ready anytime you didn't know what to read next.

"Hello, Laura!" A friendly nod followed before the librarian returned to her work. Slowly Laura walked along the rows of books. She loved the smell of paper, as well as the reverent silence that reigned in these high, spacious rooms. Laura loved to come here. Ever since she had learned to read, books were more to her than just something you had to stick your nose into because the teacher told you to. For her, the characters in books were friends who took her on adventurous journeys to other, exciting worlds. Sometimes, when she finished reading a book and closed the lid, she was sad to have to leave her new friends.

Laura rummaged through the shelves, stroking the backs of the books in search of new reading material; in search of a new world in which she could immerse herself to forget her own one for a while. She finally found what she was looking for in the books for young people, took a promising title from the shelf and went to one of the seating that were everywhere in the library. Cozy armchairs invited to read and Laura grabbed one of them. Sighing, she let herself fall into it, put her bag next to it and opened her book. She had picked 'Dead girls don't lie'. *And dead girls don't giggle*, she thought the moment she started reading.

At first she found it difficult to concentrate on the content. Again and again her thoughts returned to what had just happened. She didn't know what was actually worse: that Tobi had laughed at her or that her best friend had participated. But soon the story had captured her completely and Laura only looked up again when an older man sat in the opposite chair. For a moment their gazes met before she looked into the book again. She had seen him before when he read stories to a few smaller children and she knew he was called 'Grandpa

Anton'. He didn't seem that old yet. Although he was bald, she didn't think he was much older than her father. At least he wasn't as wrinkly as she would expect from a real grandfather. From the corner of her eye Laura noticed Grandpa Anton inspecting her from head to toe while he nervously looked around. He was holding a newspaper, but he wasn't reading it. He cleared his throat loudly several times, which made her look up again. Once, when she looked up, he nodded somehow meaningfully over to the shelves. She followed his gaze and let hers wander along the long rows of books. A single reader was about to put a book back on the shelf. A little further away, at the other end of the room, she could see Mrs. Stemmler, who had made herself comfortable in an armchair near the exit and was leafing through a magazine. Apart from that the library seemed rather abandoned at the moment, as Laura noticed. She was overcome by a strange, unpleasant feeling. What was that shit about?

# April 10, 2017

Back home again, Tatjana peels herself out of her grey coat, which she carefully puts up at the coat rack. Afterward—following the usual, trained and convulsively maintained procedures—she wants to exchange her street shoes for slippers that she wears in the house. The shoes are wet and dirty. The mud from the construction site further down the road and the water that soaked the shoes as she stepped into a puddle now form a new one at her feet.

Following a sudden impulse, she decides differently and starts to run all the way through the house, up the polished stairs to her daughter's room. In the meticulously tidy girl's room she throws herself onto the bed and kicks her shoes off her feet, watches as they land on the snow-white runner in the middle of the room and the dirty water leaves ugly stains. She also pulls off her wet socks, leaving them lying in front of the bed as a messy wet heap.

Tatjana buries her nose in her pillow, takes a deep breath. But there is nothing of Laura anymore. No hair on the pillow, no trace of her scent, not even a small, at least weakly perceptible whiff of her has remained. On the day her daughter disappeared, Tatjana had freshly covered the bed, as she did every week. Only much too late, when the laundry had long since been washed, did Tatjana realize that she had thus destroyed the last remaining trace of Laura's smell. She misses her daughter's scent. She misses it. She misses Laura! A thin sob comes from Tatjana's throat.

She remains lying for a moment, needs a minute to compose herself and to fight down the tears that rise inside her. But then she gets up, exits the room and leaves the door half-open, so that you can still see the chaos and the trail leading to the bed. She carefully tries to avoid stepping on the traces she left behind and goes back to the coat rack to put on her slippers. After that she goes to the kitchen where she boils water and starts peeling potatoes for dinner. During the dull activity she tries not to think of anything. But the silence around her, only quietly interrupted by the water that slowly begins to bubble, makes her thoughts buzz louder through her head.

"'mash 'tatoes!" The memory of a bell-like voice and little fingers reaching for the hot hotplate is flashing through her mind. Piercing pain comes along with it, because she hasn't heard this voice for too long. She quickly tries to push away the thought of the anxious question of whether she will ever hear that voice again. Or her laughter. Since Laura is gone, there's not much laughing here. She has to try to hold on to hope. Maybe someone will see the missing person announcement. Someone who has seen her. Someone who knows where she is. Tatjana thinks of the encounter in the park in the afternoon, which she found strange. Sometimes during her walks she talks to people, asks if they have seen the girl and then always points to Laura's photo. Most of the time people hardly look at it, but if they do, they stop for a moment and then say a few compassionate, regretful and encouraging phrases. Today she showed the picture to a man sitting on one of the park benches. He also looked at the missing person announcement. Instead of the expected reaction, it seemed for a moment as if he wanted to say something else. A strange, indefinable expression scurried across his face before he said in a rushed tone: "Sorry, I'm in a hurry." Then he stood up and hurried away.

Her hands do the work mechanically. Finally she pauses because she notices that she peels far too many potatoes for just two people. Tatjana slices the potatoes smaller, adds salt to the foaming water and lets the slices slide in. Later she wants to make fresh mashed potatoes out of them. Her daughter loved to eat it when she was a baby. Another flash of memory. A laughing face smeared with puree. Recently there has often been mashed potatoes.

She covers the pot with its lid and leaves the kitchen. Goes back up to the upper floor, where the door to the children's room at the end of the corridor is still half-open. But she doesn't want to go in there. Instead, she opens the door that leads to her reading room. With a groan she moves the wing chair from its traditional place, pushes it into the door frame and sits down. She can see everything from here. The entrance of the house with the coat rack at the foot of the staircase, the descending stairs and the upper floor. Her gaze clings to the mud tracks she has laid, follows their path to the end of the hallway and stops on her shoes. She stares at this stain until it blurs before her eyes, becomes unclear and mixes with the fantasy that Laura had finally come home.

\*\*\*

Two hours later, when the front door opens again, there is a biting stench in the air. It smells burned. Gray smoke from the kitchen fills the hallway. Jochen is instantly pervaded by panic.

"Damn! Tatjana!"

An adrenalin-soaked split second is enough to transport a flood of information through his body. Where there's smoke, there's fire! Danger! He mustn't lose her!

Pressing the sleeve of his jacket in front of his face, he opens the kitchen door. Biting smoke wafts towards him, cloaks him and immediately irritates his eyes. Jochen instinctively hurries to the kitchen window, which he can hardly see through the smoky fog. He doesn't have to be able to see it to know where it is. Coughing, he opens it wide. The moment he hears the insulation strip coming off the frame with a smacking noise, a sequence from a film shoots through his head. Superficial knowledge about sudden oxygen supply and jets of flames, flickering flames licking from ceilings. In a split second, his mental cinema shows him the exploding penthouse of a tall building, a flaming, destructive inferno, and he almost expects everything to blow up in his face.

Instead, fresh air simply flows into the room. Coughing, he sticks his head out of the window, fills his lungs, takes a deep breath before stopping again, turns around and stares into the smoky room. He can spot a pot on the stove as the source of the smoke, so he grabs it and painfully burns his fingers on the hot metal. Jochen screams in pain, but doesn't just let go of the pot, but throws it out the window without further ado. There he takes another deep breath before his gaze searches the kitchen again. No trace of Tatjana. Slowly the room clears up. Jochen's panic also gradually subsides. Instead, anger germinates inside him. Where the hell is his wife while the house almost burns down?

The air in the kitchen is still stuffy and a painful blister is slowly bulging in his right palm. He turns off the

28

red hot plate, leaves the room and closes the kitchen door. Let's air it out first. The burnt skin should be cooled. Frozen peas? No, he doesn't want to go back to the kitchen. Perhaps there's burn ointment upstairs in the bathroom.

Jochen turns to the stairs and sees the dirty marks leading upward. For a moment, his heart almost stops again. His daughter was the only one who dared to walk through the house with her dirty shoes. First with child-like, then with adolescent ignorance of parental regulations.

The blister is instantly forgotten, the pain in his hand is suppressed by the spontaneous thought that his child might have come home after all. A dam breaks inside him, a barrier that protects him from his feelings and which he laboriously had set up to live on. The sight of the dirty footsteps lets emotions befall him, hopes and desires that he no longer allowed himself, because the disappointment would be too big if they were not fulfilled. The spark of hope blazes in him, which he thought had long been suffocated. Taking several stairs at once, he runs upstairs – and freezes when he arrives at the top.

It's not a horrible sight to look at, but it's terrible anyway. He has found Tatjana. She just sits there, her legs pulled close to her upper body. His wife seems to be frozen in a fetal sitting posture, with an apathetic gaze into emptiness. Jochen doesn't have to follow it at all, he doesn't have to look into the nursery to know that the traces don't mean anything good. Tatjana doesn't even seem to notice him. As suddenly as hope has come over him, it is washed away by another flood that leaves nothing but despair.

Without addressing his wife, he walks past her into the bathroom, loudly slams the door behind him, leans his forehead against that of his reflection in the mirror and cools his blister with running cold water.

***

Later in the evening they sit together on the sofa and the loudly blaring TV cannot hide the unpleasant silence between them. They both lack the words to express their own pain to the other without the unspoken reproach they make to each other. The accusation that the other doesn't find the right magic words to alleviate his own suffering. Ever since their daughter didn't come home anymore, they're alone with this pain, each for themselves. And each of them has their own way of dealing with it.

While they sit silently next to each other, Tatjana thinks about the burnt potatoes. Jochen just tries to concentrate on the soccer match and doesn't think at all. Only when a player of his team loses the ball to his opponent he interrupts the silence to grumpily proclaim that the player is a jerk. Tatjana doesn't listen at all. Although she also stares at the screen, she only notices little of the match. Meanwhile she's not only afraid for her daughter, but also for herself. Only the loud slamming of the door when Jochen went into the bathroom had ripped her from her thoughts earlier. Only then did she notice the stench in the apartment. Before that she was ... somehow far out. She stood up, clumsily, with rusty limbs, staggering to the bathroom door. There she put her hand on the door handle, her ear on the wood, unsure whether she should enter. She decided against it, went downstairs instead. Without looking into the kitchen first, she opened the front door, determinedly left the house, picked up the pot that lay in the bed under the kitchen window. Subconsciously, she was aware of what was going on around her. A small part of her had stayed awake, but the great rest of her mind had retreated to a place within herself, where everything seemed soft, warm and muffled and felt as if you were dozing, as if a fever was paralyzing the body. A place that puts you to sleep like a lullaby, that captures you and that you can hardly leave once you've reached it. A place where you want to stay while life around you burns to ashes. She was incapable, unable to release herself from her numbness – not even when she smelled the smoke.

What could be shaken out of the pot without any aids, she threw into the trash can. She took the pot, in which a black crust of burnt potatoes stuck, back into the house. She was about to scrub it clean with a wire brush when Jochen came into the kitchen. He sat down at the large dining table which occupied half of the kitchen, and looked at her silently. His gaze rested perceptibly on her neck. She doubled her efforts, scrubbed even more vigorously, but the damn pot didn't get clean. Finally the silence became too much for her, tugged at her nerves too much, so she turned around jerkily and took the word: "I'll probably have to boil the pot with sauerkraut to loosen the burnt crust."

Jochen shrugged indifferently.

"I actually wanted to make mashed potatoes for us," she told him somewhat helplessly. Again she got only a shrug as an answer. She made one last attempt to start a conversation: "I should order pizza. What do you like for topping?"

"Salami," was his simple answer. And although there was so much to say, their conversation was limited to those few words.

# March 9, 2016

Adelheid Stemmler later remembered exactly what she could observe on the afternoon of March 6, 2016. She had an excellent memory for names and faces and had known the girl for quite some time. Today, a few days after their last encounter, she read about her disappearance in the newspaper. Immediately all her alarm bells were ringing and she had a horrible suspicion.

Laura had come around 4:30 pm, when Adelheid was just about to sort in a few returned works. She seemed as cheerful as ever to the librarian, immediately set out on her own search for a new book, and by the time Mrs. Stemmler had finished shelving, Laura had apparently already found what she was looking for. Otherwise it was quiet this afternoon, only a few readers were in the library. She knew most of them personally, even if only fleetingly. Since there wasn't much to do, Adelheid took one of the magazines on display and made herself comfortable in an armchair near the lending desk. She saw Laura sitting a bit away in one of the armchairs, her nose buried deep in a book. Adelheid was soon engrossed in an interesting article, yet she registered, albeit only marginally, that Anton Wacholski sat with the girl. She knew him as a big reader. Some time ago he had a serious car accident and during his convalescence he had become a regular guest in her halls. A limping and an always slightly bent posture had remained from a spinal injury, which together with his hair loss made him look older than he actually was. In Adelheid's eyes, Wacholski wasn't an attractive man, but a pleasant, courteous visitor. Due to pain, he couldn't do much more than sit around and read for a long time. It turned out that he had a real talent for captivating the little visitors with his full-sounding voice, and soon many of the children knew him as the nice *Grandpa Anton* who read them great stories. Despite the fact that he was slowly getting better, he came two or three times a week and was almost part of Adelheid's inventory. Only now, against the background that a child had disappeared immediately after it had been in her library, his commitment suddenly seemed questionable to her.

Looking back, she remembered that after Grandpa Anton had taken a seat, it didn't take long for Laura to wriggle about on her chair, increasingly restless. She also remembered the way Laura stood up shortly afterward, almost rushing towards the exit after he had leaned forward and said something to her that Adelheid couldn't hear from her position. The girl seemed restless, hectic, in retrospect perhaps even anxious. She had suddenly been in a terrible hurry to borrow her book and leave. As soon as they had completed the formalities for the lending, she had hurried to the exit.

She hadn't considered the matter important that day. Only when she learned of Laura's disappearance a few days later did Adelheid reproach herself bitterly for apparently misjudging the situation. She had thought the girl was in a hurry and hadn't even had the idea that something might be wrong. Immediately afterward Anton Wacholski had left as well, and although it seemed unimportant at that time, this was perhaps the crucial clue the police needed to find the girl. Adelheid Stemmler picked up the phone.

# March 6, 2016

Grandpa Anton's dubious gestures unsettled Laura and created an uncomfortable feeling. He behaved really weird. What did he want from her? Finally he leaned over to her and asked in a whisper: "Tell me, girl, are you here alone or do you have an admirer who accompanies you?"

Laura looked around. Apart from Mrs. Stemmler, who sat far away, there was nobody here. Only the young man who now leaned against one of the shelves and read the blurb of a book. He looked vaguely familiar to her, even though she couldn't tell at first glance where they had met before. She briefly asked herself whether he might be able to help her if the strange old man continued to bother her, or whether she should go to Mrs. Stemmler and ask her for help. Laura decided for a quick retreat instead. Without saying a word, she closed her book and went straight to the lending desk. The old man was probably one of those perverts you'd better stay away from. She wouldn't let a guy like that talk her into something! His gaze followed her as hers fell on the clock above the exit. Shit, just after six! She hadn't even noticed that so much time had passed.

She hectically calculated the departure times of the buses. How long did the bus always take from where she usually got on it? Could be tight. Nevertheless, she put the book and her card on the lending desk. She waited, impatiently stepping from one leg to the other, until the librarian scanned it and handed the book back to her. Laura just stepped outside when the brake lights of the bus went out. The bus stop was right across the street. She quickly looked around. When she saw that no car

was coming, she started to run, waving her arms violently as she crossed the street, hoping the bus driver would
look in the rear-view mirror and interpret her signals
correctly. But the bus left.

"Shit! It's not my lucky day," she snorted in frustration as she watched the missed ride. A glance at the
timetable and her cell phone told her that the next bus
would arrive in about one hour. Also, there was a text
message waiting to be read.

"Hey sweetie, why did you run away?" Kerstin wanted
to know. Quickly she wrote back: *It really sucked that you
made fun of me with the others!*

It felt good to express her anger. So, as soon as the
first message was sent, she typed another one: *… and the
way you approached Tobi was really slutty.*

*You want something from Tobi? Btw, chill, luv u!*, came back
promptly. Three more hastily typed messages were
needed to correct this erroneous impression and to signal absolute disinterest in the object of her desire. Only
then did she call her mother to ask if she could pick her
up.

"Unfortunately, your credit is not sufficient for another call. Please top up your card and then try again," a
computer voice informed her friendly, instead of con-
necting Laura.

*Damn, everything's going wrong today!* Actually, she should
be home in half an hour at the latest. She could go back
to the library and wait there for the next bus, but then
the trouble with her parents would be inevitable. And
was even less in the mood for this strange Grandpa Anton than for a long walk. If she hurried, she might even
make it in time without getting trouble at home.

She shivered. The sun was already setting and its rays
that were already warming during the day impressively

illuminated the sky, turning it pink, purple and deep red, but the temperature had already dropped considerably. If only she'd listened to her mother, who had told her as always to take her jacket with her. But when Laura had left the house, a nice warm day seemed to be ahead, so she had disregarded the good advice. *Never mind*, she thought with a shrug, *walking will warm me up*. She quickly pulled her headphones out of her pocket and plugged them into her cell phone. So she could at least use the stupid thing as an MP3 player if it wouldn't let her make a phone call. A moment later, the music of her current favorite band roared loudly in her ears. Laura put on the hood of her sweatshirt, adjusted her steps to the beat and marched off.

She didn't look back. She was too lost in her thoughts, which were still about Tobi, Kerstin and the embarrassment she had endured. After walking a few minutes, an approaching car slowed down and drove beside her at walking pace. The window on the passenger's side lowered. Confused, she slowed her own pace, pulled the plugs out of her ears and took a look inside. Laura was frightened. The strange man from the library looked back at her.

"Hey girl," Grandpa Anton shouted. "Where are you going?"

She didn't know why she even replied to him when she said, "Home."

"You shouldn't be walking around alone outside at this hour. It's getting dark already. Should I take you with me?"

Without saying a word, she shook her head and walked on. She wished he would just drive off and leave her alone, but he didn't make it that easy for her. Although he had to realize that she wouldn't talk to him and certainly wouldn't get into his car, he continued to roll slowly next to her.

"Where do you live?"

He sounded worried and friendly, but from an early age she had been warned not to talk to strangers, not to accept gifts from them and not to go with them at all. Even without these warnings, Laura wouldn't have gotten into the car. Instinctively she did not trust the guy.

"It's not far anymore, I'm almost there," she quickly lied. Actually she hadn't even made a third of the way yet, but she wouldn't get in the car with this guy! Slowly a vague feeling of fear crept up inside her. She accelerated her steps as Grandpa Anton's car continued to roll next to her.

"But maybe it would be better if I chauffeured you the rest of the way. You never know who else is on the street …"

He didn't finish his sentence, because Laura cut off his word. With more courage in her voice than she would have dared, she yelled at him, "Are you a fucking pervert who picks up little kids on the street and takes them to the woods? You've already stared at me so oddly in the library. Just leave me alone!"

She moved away from the vehicle as far as the narrow sidewalk allowed. Despite her aggressive tone, she got more and more scared. The guy didn't let up. "No, I just wanted to make sure you get home okay. In the library, I already wanted to draw your attention to the fact that …"

Again, she wouldn't let him finish. "Fuck off!" Laura screamed angrily and anxiously at the same time, before she took her heels and ran off. "Leave me alone!"

The car next to her also accelerated.

# March 9, 2016

Police Sergeant Likar was sitting at his desk thinking about the current missing person's case.

"Most runaways reappear very quickly on their own," he had reassured the woman when she called his office in her first concern. Tatjana Wenz wasn't the first mother Likar had to calm down in the course of his life as a civil servant because her beloved offspring hadn't arrived in time for dinner. According to Mrs. Wenz, her thirteen-year-old daughter Laura should have been home hours ago. The concerned mother had already called all her child's friends and asked if Laura was with them or if they knew where she might be. A girl named Kerstin told her about an argument she had had in the afternoon, that Laura had run away afterward and later called her friend again by text message.

But Kerstin didn't know either where Laura was now. Of course Mrs. Wenz had also tried it on her daughter's mobile phone before, but after several ringings, the call was simply rejected and there was only the mailbox. Mrs. Wenz told all this hectically, completely out of her mind from worry. The officer had shown understanding for her situation, but from many years of professional experience he knew that such cases usually solved themselves after only a few hours, because the defiant teenager got hungry and quickly stood on the parental doorstep again.

"Please calm down!" Likar had interrupted her flow of speech. "I'm sure you worry for nothing. Or would you think of a reason why your daughter should run away? Was there an argument at home?"

A moment of silence on the phone had told him that he probably hadn't been wrong with this assumption. And the audible confirmation followed, "Yes, a few days ago we had an argument. But that was really completely irrelevant. Laura wouldn't ..."

"Mrs. Wenz," the sergeant had cut in, "you said your daughter is thirteen. That's the classic age for such adolescent escapades. Even a harmless argument can lead to incredibly stubborn reactions in teenagers. I'm sure she'll soon ..."

"Damn, how can you be so sure? You don't know my daughter! Something must have happened to Laura! I want you to move your lazy ass right now and please ..."

"Hold your horses, Mrs. Wenz!" the officer had taken control of the conversation again. "I understand your anxiety, but you gotta calm down and be rational. We cannot go on like this. For how many hours exactly has your daughter disappeared now?"

"She should have been home at seven and now it's almost half past ten."

"Mrs. Wenz, that's only just three hours. Maybe your daughter has a boyfriend you don't know, and she's with him and has forgotten about time."

"If Laura had a boyfriend, I'd know about it. Something *must* have happened to her!" The mother didn't let up.

"What about the girl's father? Are you separated? Could your daughter perhaps be with him?" was his next assumption.

"No! My husband and I have been happily married for seventeen years," was the piqued reply.

"Well then." The excitement seemed completely in vain to Likar, but since the missing person was still so

40

young and her mother wouldn't give in anyway, he asked her to come by the precinct. He had sighed when he finally hung up the phone. That was all he needed. The office was chronically understaffed, he himself already worked the third week of night shift and the additional on-call duty last weekend had minimized his leisure time even further. The prospect of spending half the night torturing himself with a mother on the verge of a nervous breakdown just because her offspring was a little late didn't exactly make him happy.

Less than twenty minutes later, the excited woman had stood at the precinct's door. Concern was written all over her face, accompanied by smeared mascara, testifying recent tears of anxiety. Likar let her in and wrote the missing person's report. Outwardly he kept calm, but inwardly he had cursed the unnecessary paperwork that now accrued. When it was finally done, he had given the colleagues on patrol a description of Laura via police radio – with the request to look for the girl.

"That's all we can do for the moment. I suggest you go home now. Maybe your girl will be home by the time you arrive. Then please don't forget to inform us in your joy. Not that we send a group of hundred in search of your daughter while she's already sleeping peacefully in her bed." At that moment Likar also wished a comfortable bed for himself and suppressed a yawn. With a laboriously maintained smile he had complimented the woman out the door.

The next morning, when Laura still hadn't shown up, his colleagues on duty had put together a search party. As usual with missing minors, the police and countless volunteers searched the area on a large scale. Several pieces of forest were meticulously combed and divers were sent on a mission to search the murky waters of a nearby lake. They located the girl's mobile phone and found it in a garbage can at the train station. It seemed quite possible that Laura had just thrown it away before she boarded a train. The officers couldn't help but interrogate the parents. Did Laura have distant friends or relatives she might go to? Or an acquaintance on the Internet? Someone she would turn to if she had problems?

Likar thought feverishly, turning and turning the few facts gathered so far. Then he was suddenly torn from his thoughts. The phone rang. Likar answered. At the other end of the line was Adelheid Stemmler and gave a hint that could bring the breakthrough in the investigation. When Likar hung up the phone, his hope rose that they would soon find Laura and bring her back home.

# April 10, 2017

With her eyes wide open Tatjana lies next to her husband and stares into the darkness. It's quiet in the house, only his snoring interrupts the silence – and the annoying ticking of the clock, which comes almost inaudibly from the hallway. Tick – tick – tick. Every second, it accompanies her restless thoughts with this quiet sound that slowly drives her mad. Again and again, her brain plays back the past, dissects it, analyses it, tries to draw conclusions about the present from it, while the seconds elapse audibly. *Where's my child?*

At first she couldn't believe Laura had just run away. She wouldn't do such a thing, there was no reason at all.

Something must have happened to her. Tatjana had scolded the officer. She had almost called this Likar an idiot, who should believe her and do something. A police radio message to his colleagues seemed far too little to her, a search party the next day far too late. Why didn't they immediately use all available resources?

Meanwhile, however, she clings to the hope that her daughter had simply run away. This idea makes it a bit easier, although it's accompanied by bitter self-reproaches. Maybe sometimes they should have been a little less strict. Allow her to put on some make-up or buy the short skirt she liked. The one to which Tatjana had said a motherly, strict No, because she knew exactly how Laura's father would have reacted. It was hard for him to get used to the idea that his little girl was slowly growing up. *But he can get used to the idea that she's dead*, she thinks angrily and accusingly, succumbing to the temptation to seek Jochen's guilt. There had been no other conflicts. Nothing that would explain why Laura ran away and left her in fear and worry without at least leaving an explanatory letter or sending a sign of life. Part of her knows that it's absurd to believe that these harmless arguments could really be the cause. Sometimes she even catches herself eyeing Jochen suspiciously. Didn't he just want to protect her and preserve her childhood a little longer? Was there something else behind it that he wanted to keep the boys away from his daughter? In all her years together, such a thought had never occurred to her. But wasn't Jochen just a man? The passion in her marriage had died over the years; replaced by a deep intimacy, which she no longer feels since the life that connected them both was missing. Their relationship can't be defined as sexually debauched. Even before Laura disappeared, they hadn't slept together for a long time. *Laura was—no, is!—such a pretty girl. Is! Undoubtedly blooming, maturing. Did Jochen do something he never should have done?*

The next moment she feels guilty because she thinks such thoughts at all. Her brain is afraid to formulate the thought in all its clarity, but it is still there. How can she? Hasn't Jochen been faithfully standing by her side for almost two decades? Reliable, loyal – a decent man who has always taken good care of his family!

The police also came up with such thoughts. Laura's parents' house was searched, as was the garage and the shed in the garden. They hadn't been treated unkindly, though.

"You're not under suspicion. We simply have to exclude all possibilities. Of course we understand that this is unpleasant for you, an invasion of your privacy, but we have to look around the house. Do we have your permission or do we need a search warrant?"

She will never forget what it felt like to be unjustly suspected. In spite of all the kindness, they were given this feeling. It was as if they were to blame that Laura was no longer there. It had been pitifully and respectfully claimed that the search of their house was quite normal and couldn't be avoided, but Jochen and Tatjana had nevertheless felt as if they were suspected of having done something to their beloved child. The officers meticulously turned her house upside down and left behind nothing but chaos.

Tatjana keeps staring at the ceiling and listens to her husband's quiet snoring. Jochen has changed a lot in the last year. Deep worry lines mark his face today, he looks tired, emaciated, even on weekends when he has slept long. The man who used to always make her laugh now

44

has something sad about him – like a clown who perish-es in the circus ring every day and yet is aware of his duty to catch the flying cake with his face. When was the last time they really laughed together?

She's aware they're just living side-by-side. Suffering comrades who endure the common fate together but are alone. She lacks the former togetherness but also the strength to change something about building a bridge where there is now a deep gap. At the beginning, in the first days after Laura's disappearance, they still clung to each other and tried to hold each other. But with each passing day the confidence crumbled. Hope melted away like snow in spring. As it melted, the connection between them was hollowed out, as if it were made of brittle sandstone that couldn't withstand the tides of despair. All that remained was the façade of the once solid and happy marriage.

In these eleven months Tatjana felt Jochen withdraw-ing more and more. If he didn't want to completely lose his secure position in life, he had to look ahead. He had to function, do his job and couldn't afford to sink into a sea of grief. He was a realist. Just like his wife, he didn't believe that Laura had just run away. And one day he even said, "As hard as it is, Tatjana, we have to face the facts: Laura is probably dead."

This thought was logical, rational – but the feeling that accompanied it was unbearable for Tatjana. It clasped her chest. There was a feeling of tightness, as if this most terrible of thoughts would sit on her ribs – ready to pierce them to stop her heart. Even though they had no absolute certainty, there was almost no oth-er possible explanation. When Jochen spoke it out loud for the first time, she slapped him in the face from a first reflex. From today's point of view it wasn't imaginable. Later she apologized for it.

Since then, they have talked about it countless times, arguing about it before finally silently burying the subject. In the meantime they hardly mention Laura's name anymore. Nevertheless—or because of this—the subject is constantly unspoken between them. Actually, Tatjana has to admit that Jochen is right. But deep down inside she knows that her child must be out there somewhere. Alive. She doesn't want to believe anything else. Without certainty she can ... no, she may not allow herself any other thoughts. It would cost her her mind.

Like that ticking. Tick – tick – tick ...

Seconds that seep away irretrievably.

*Irretrievably.* A cruel word that stabs her in the heart. The feeling of having lost everything she used to live for and what she loved is hardly bearable. Even the man next to her is only a shadow of the past. A fading image, a caricature of himself. Just like her. Stoically, day after day, she follows her routines so that she has something to do – apart from slowly going crazy. *I don't seem to be far away from insanity anymore,* she assesses her situation. Her body is tired to death, exhausted beyond its limits, but her mind behaves like a cat that spins around trying to bite its own tail. The carousel in her head always leads her back to the same thoughts and conclusions – like a perpetuum mobile that never stands still.

Tick ... tick ... tick ...

Once again, dull rage mixes with her despair. Anger at her helplessness, at Jochen, the police, at the neighbors who saw nothing. Anger at herself because she can't do anything but hope and nail these damn posters to trees just so the wind or a passer-by can tear them down again. She is even angry at the innocent man who was

46

wrongly suspected at the beginning. She almost wishes he hadn't been able to credibly free himself from suspicion. Then they would have at least a culprit. Then she'd have someone who's responsible instead of having just this agonizing uncertainty. She's angry because she can do nothing but stare into the darkness. She can't even sleep. She can't turn back time, she can only lie there and somehow kill it.

*Time.* This damn ticking's driving her crazy!

Following a new impulse, she gets up, waddles through the bedroom on bare soles, stirs up her anger when she hits her toe at the protruding corner post of the bed. She suppresses a strong curse because she doesn't want to wake up Jochen. Quietly and self-controlled, she closes the bedroom door behind her. She goes into the bathroom, presses a switch and looks at her pale reflection in the faint neon light. A sad, lean face looks back at her, with the dark rings under her eyes, surrounded by stringy hanging hair. Damn, what has become of her? She sees an old woman looking at her instead of the fun-loving, attractive woman she was a year ago.

Tears gather in her tired eyes. When was the last time she really slept? She feels at the end of her strength and yet too tense to sleep. As if life would run out of her like the sand of an hourglass. The feeling of not being able to live like this for another day becomes almost overwhelming. Her gaze wanders over the razor blades, which the manufacturer has foresightedly coated with a thin, protective wire mesh to prevent injuries. Another thought she doesn't want to allow herself is trying to force its way into her tired mind. She quickly pushes it aside. *Perhaps a hot bath will help me,* she thinks instead. Tatjana turns to the bathtub, puts the plug into the drain and opens the tap. Lost in thought, she watches for a moment as the warm steaming water pour in before taking off her nightgown and sliding in. She lets the tub run full, then turns the tap off again and leans back. But as soon as the noise of the flowing water no longer drowns out the silence, she hears the ticking again. Actually only very quietly, but nevertheless it echoes in her ears. Overloud.

Tick ... tick ... tick ...

It's impossible to find peace.

She gets out of the tub again and wraps herself in a towel. Then, on wet soles, she purposefully walks down into the dining room, grabs a chair and drags it up the stairs. Puts it against the wall, climbs on it and stretches out to get to the damn thing. This acrobatics is necessary because Jochen, who is much taller than she is, fixed the clock a bit to the left of the wall above the steps, where she can't place the chair directly underneath. If she falls, she will surely break her neck. Right now she wouldn't give a shit. Tatjana's feet are still wet and she almost slips off the smooth leather cover during her daring action, but manages to keep her balance and reach the clock. She clamps the loot under her arm, goes back into the bathroom and throws it into the tub. With a feeling of satisfaction she watches the timepiece sinking down. The second hand makes one last move before the troublemaker finally dies. Now she has just drowned the time. In a moment she will do the same with her grief. And she decides at that moment that tomorrow she will change something. She will take back her life!

Tatjana sneaks down into the kitchen, takes a big sip from the open bottle of wine that she otherwise only uses for cooking. Then another one. Only when the

bottle is empty does she go back to bed, where she finally falls into a deep calm sleep.

# March 6, 2016

"Fuck off!" the girl yelled. Her instincts were wide awake. Nevertheless, it had been more than easy for him to nab her. A little bit of violence had been necessary because she had tried to fight back. A few strong punches made her dazed. Physically, he was so far superior to her that it hadn't been a big problem to get her under control and take her where he wanted her. It had happened spontaneously when the opportunity presented itself, which he couldn't have planned better.

It's a good thing he followed her that afternoon. He almost believed in destiny because she had to walk today and took this path. A heap of luck for him and bad luck for the girl. The old guy in his Mercedes and his own manipulation skills had made this possible. The old man had noticed in the library that Tom had been watching the girl. But his attempt to address her and warn her about him had only made him appear strange and dubious. Tom had watched Laura stand up and flee. He had quickly put the book he had pretended to read back on the shelf, then waited a moment before following her. Outside he had watched her miss her bus and set off on foot. He had let a few more minutes pass, then he had followed her on his bike at some distance. Tom could see that the old man had braked and slowly drove beside Laura, so he had also slowed his pace. Unfortunately Tom couldn't hear what was being said. Too much distance. But when Laura screamed that the old man should fuck off, the wind had carried the words clearly. Then she had run away and he had pedaled again.

Sundown was already setting in and the streetlamps that weren't yet lit encouraged him to approach the girl directly. The fear in her voice showed him that if he did it cleverly now, the right time had finally come. He'd been targeting this girl for a few weeks. Facebook and other social media platforms had supplied him with a wide selection of potential victims who could be narrowed down to achievable goals by making the appropriate entries. Finally he had made a preselection and made friends with a few girls by using a specially created false profile. Most of them were quite naive. It was so easy to elicit enough information from them to reveal locations where he could inconspicuously take a first look at them. Some were stupid enough to post on their profile when they went to the movies or to eat ice cream in town. Actually, he had come for a completely different girl back then, but then he had seen her: Laura. She stood with her friends in front of a cinema, in joyful anticipation of seeing the new *Twilight*-movie, and it was love at first sight. This girl stood out from the crowd. She looked pure and unspent, renounced make-up completely and with her natural beauty she outshined the average appearance of her painted companions. He saw her and within a blink of an eye he had made his choice.

Even though he hadn't intended to watch the film, Tom bought a ticket. The afternoon show wasn't well attended. During the film he had discreetly sat down two rows behind the girls, a little further to the outside, where he had the best view. Not on the screen, but on Laura.

In the evening he searched the social networks for her account. Maybe she had particularly strict parents who didn't allow her to use Facebook, because after hours Tom still hadn't found her. But her stupid girlfriend gave enough information about herself so it wasn't too hard to find her again.

He quickly caught up and approached his victim.

"Do you need help?" he asked hypocritically when he had reached her. As the old man's car turned the next corner, Tom slowed his speed and adjusted it to Laura's steps.

It was so easy to start a conversation with Laura. She was still shocked and seemed happy about his presence. Trustingly she told him immediately about the pervert who had just turned her on. She was excited, out of breath and happy that someone had joined her and that she was no longer alone. She felt relieved that the supposed threat was gone. Absolutely blind to the new and only danger.

"That's weird! When I hear something like that, I'm really glad I'm not a sweet girl like you!" he commented on her experience. The compliment accompanying the remark made Laura blush. "I'd be afraid ... all alone when it gets dark."

Laura nodded, "Yes, it was creepy with that guy. He was already so weird in the library. You were there too, right?"

Shit, so she had noticed him. He quickly lied, "Yes, I was looking for a book for the university."

Tom still looked young enough to pass as a student in the last semester. When Laura asked him what he was studying, he grinned crookedly and replied: "Psychology." Then, as if he didn't already know the answer, he asked her where she had to go.

"Should I see you home? For safety's sake, in case the weirdo comes back," he offered, apparently worried, after she had told him her destination.

"Really, would you? That would be so nice of you. I was a little scared before you showed up." She gratefully accepted his offer and gave him a radiant, trusting smile.

Initially, he had thought it would be a lot harder. But it was so easy – as if he were a spider building a perfidious web. In this case Laura was the fly whose trajectory was determined by a particularly unfavorable breeze and drove her straight into the trap. Excitement went hand in hand with this unexpected development, working like a stimulant, making his throat dry and his hands wet. When she then told him how much in a hurry she was, he offered her a ride on his luggage carrier. "Sit there, then I'll drive you home," he offered with a voice that was brittle with excitement. "Could get a little bumpy, but if you hold on tight, you'll be fine. We'll be a lot faster that way."

The warm grip of her hands, which she laid loosely on his hips, had an arousing effect on him. His nervousness continued to rise as they turned into his street.

*Now or never*, he thought when he suddenly left the street, bobbed roughly across the sidewalk and turned to the house. "I know a short cut!" he shouted as he drove down the road to the back of the house. Laura had trouble keeping her balance. Her hands now clung almost painfully to his hips. Behind the house he slowed down sharply and stopped abruptly. Her grip loosened. With a frightened outcry she slipped from the carrier and fell to the ground behind the bike. Tom quickly got off his bike and let it fall carelessly into the bushes next to the stairs leading up to the back door of the house. Laura was about to jump up again. Willing to help, he reached out his hand to her, pulled her up and towards him. Laura's eyes widened. Whether from surprise or fright, he couldn't say.

"Come with me, I wanna show you something!" he said, took a few steps towards the stairs and tried to pull her with him. But Laura stopped instead – gradually her instinct reported that something was wrong. She wanted to break free, but it was too late. Before she could react or even protest, Tom turned to her and raised his hand for the first punch.

Dumbfounded, her big eyes looked into his as he punched her a second time, then a third time before she could even try to run away from him. Laura, protectively held her arms in front of her face as he hit her again. He struck hard, full of brutality, so that she staggered against the house wall. With a haymaker into the solar plexus he took her breath away. It had to go fast and it had to be effective. The adrenaline pumped through his veins as he grabbed her by the neck and hair and brutally dragged her up the stairs. His heart raced as he pulled her through the house, along the narrow hallway where she slowly caught her breath and her screams resounded. At the end of the hall he pushed Laura down the basement staircase – into the room he had prepared for her. A soiled old mattress with a latex cover lay there. He had also placed a bucket there for her nature's calls. It clattered when she hit the floor and collided with it. He had already begun the preparations weeks ago. Actually, they weren't finished yet. It was pitch dark down there, there was no lighting, at least no light switch, which you just had to flip. He didn't have time for the generator now. That's why he took the flashlight that he had deposited on the top step, switched it on and went a few steps downstairs.

The sharp beam of light cut through the darkness. From the ceiling, attached to a massive drainpipe, hung an iron chain, at the end of which a shackle shimmered dimly in the light. Then the beam was directed at the girl, who jumped at him with an inarticulate scream. She tried to scratch him, slip past him and run back up the narrow, steep basement stairs. The little beast was damn quick. She had picked herself up in a flash. He gave her another blow and violently pushed her away so that she fell again. And then she lay still, bleeding from a small laceration on her temple. Now he could tie her up without any problems. He pulled her from the foot of the stairs over to the mattress, put the flashlight on the floor and fastened the ankle shackle hanging from the ceiling around her right ankle. He secured it with a padlock that had been hanging open and waiting. Tom had deposited the key in the generator room. He wouldn't need it too often, but he shouldn't lose it either. After the lock was snapped in and he didn't have to fear any more escape attempts, he left Laura lying there, took the flashlight and went upstairs. He carefully locked the cellar door before going into the kitchen, dropping himself onto one of the old worn chairs and pulling a pack of cigarettes and a lighter out of his hip bag. Greedily, he lit a ciggy, inhaled deeply, and with each puff his excited pulse calmed down.

Shit, he really did it! He could hardly believe it himself. Despite all the preparation time that had preceded the act, he couldn't believe that he really had the courage. He had been planning his action for a long time and had now surprised himself with the implementation.

Since he could wank, he had imagined having a girl in his hands. His fantasies were sadistic, had little in common with what his girlfriend, if he ever had one, thought of as 'making love'. He liked the harder way, needed the feeling of being the boss. The daddy who really gave it to the little bitch. Once he had crossed the border to Poland and visited a whorehouse, where you could buy almost anything for little more than pocket money. But a paid slave who only did it for money, possibly even living out her inclinations, hadn't satisfied his needs. The fear in their eyes wasn't real, the submissiveness was only simulated, not forced. A hint of lust had mixed into her begging and pleading. He wanted a willing victim, but for him the attraction lay also in submission and education. It wouldn't have harmed the play if the hooker had resisted a little at first. He had beaten her and fucked her anyway, and he had climaxed, but actually she had disgusted him. The whore hadn't been worth the money.

This time it would be different.

His breath was still fast. A delicious mixture of excitement and anticipation flooded him. This time it would feel right. Damn, that was awesome! A feeling of power that he hadn't known before came along with it. But already in the next moment he got afraid of his courage. What if someone had seen him after all? What if he was caught? Damn, you could get a life sentence for something like that.

The fact that deep inside he was a wretched coward now came to the fore and was the reason why he started to ponder. Had he made a mistake? He thought over the situation again. Remembered how she had looked at him with her big, skeptical looking eyes as she pulled her plug out of her ear to hear what he had to say. Panic flooded Tom as he realized that the brat still had her cell phone. FUCK! He rushed to the cellar door, unlocked it with sweaty hands and ran down the stairs. He was in such a hurry to correct his mistake that he even forgot the flashlight upstairs. He fumbled his way in the dark, his arm stretched out and his feet shuffling – towards

56

the mattress in the corner. He felt her warm body that didn't shy away from him. She was probably still unconscious. His fingers searched hastily, palpating her clothes until he felt the mobile phone through her jeans and hastily pulled it out. He felt relieved. Then his fingers moved up to her budding breasts, sliding under her sweatshirt. He took a first taste of what now belonged to him alone. Damn, the little bitch felt awesome! Her flesh was soft and firm at the same time, enticing, very different from the worn, sagging breasts he got to see day after day at work. But then he pulled himself together and let go of her. Not like that. He wanted to really enjoy their first time and see her while they did it. First he had to provide light down here.

*Had I known that our rendezvous was today, I would have bought candles*, he thought with a smug grin as he searched his way back up.

He had walked halfway up the basement stairs when the cell phone in his hand started ringing. 'Mama' the flashing display told him. He hastily rejected the call, turned the phone off and was more than happy that he'd noticed his mistake in time. That had just gone well again. From now on he had to be extremely careful. He would later dispose of the cell phone. At the station perhaps. Then you would think the girl had run away and thrown it away before she got on a train.

This time he had been impulsive and had seized the unique opportunity, although he was still in the stage of preparation and observation. From now on, however, he would make up a plan, think carefully about his future course of action and stick exactly to it. Tom finally possessed what he had always dreamed of. Now he had to keep everything under control. By no means could he afford another stupid beginner's mistake. Carefully he

57

locked the cellar door again and sought relaxation with another cigarette. First of all calm down. Clear your head.

***

Down in the basement, Laura slowly regained consciousness. Pitch-black darkness surrounded her and she had no idea where she was and what had happened. Her first thought, *Did I fall asleep and had a nightmare?*

Her head hurt, as did her body. For a moment she was completely disoriented. Uncertain, she palpated around, feeling a soft, rubber-like surface, cold concrete floor next to it.

*Where the hell am I?*

To her left was a wall of wooden slats. A splinter of wood painfully drilled into her palm. A soft painful sound came from her throat, which felt dry and rough. Carefully she sat up, wanted to pull her knees against her body and caused a metallic clang in the middle of the movement.

*What was that?*

Her hands were touching an ankle shackle and a chain. She pulled at it. Slowly the memory of what had happened before she awoke here returned. And then Laura started to scream.

# April 11, 2017

It's already noon when Tatjana opens her eyes. A ray of sunlight tickles her awake as she turns to the window side of the room. She blinks, stretches herself. She enjoys the feeling of slowly waking up and feels unusually refreshed. For the first time in a long while, she feels rested after a good sleep. Today she slowly finds her way into the day and only then—and not as the very first thing—Laura comes to her mind. Even now the thought is painful, but it is less like a waking slap in the face. She manages to push it aside and notices instead that it's a beautiful, sunny day. While she has often gone down to the kitchen lately to light a cigarette—she started smoking a few months ago—she first goes to the bathroom today. There she looks at the sunken clock. Jochen had either not noticed it at all when he was in the bathroom this morning, or he didn't care. In any case, he hadn't taken it out of the tub.

She steps into the shower cabinet and turns on the warm water. For a few minutes she enjoys the wet jets of water that pelt down her head, the feeling of the water running along her body, washing away the night sweat and her cloudy thoughts.

When she leaves the cabin, water vapor hangs in the air, accumulates in droplets on the frosted glass window and fogs up the mirror. She towels herself, takes a toothbrush and brushes her teeth while wiping the mirror with her other hand. For the first time in a long time she examines her mirror image in detail with a watchful eye. A soft smile plays around the corners of her mouth, although she doesn't like what she sees. She smiles because today, for the first time, she feels the inner drive that is necessary not to let this day pass as sadly and monotonously as the previous days.

*I'll go to town later*, decides Tatjana while she looks at herself. Without the burden that accompanies her otherwise. Today she won't take posters with her, she won't talk to strangers. Finally she will do something only for herself. She wants to give her appearance some of the freshness she feels today. She takes a brush, combs the wet, knotted strands until her hair is smooth and shiny. But it doesn't become less gray. A few unsightly gray strands now run through her dark hair, especially on her temples. She thinks about buying a hair tint. Yes, she will look much younger again with a little color. Tatjana feels the desire to improve herself immediately and reaches for the mascara, which she hasn't touched for a long time. When she pulls out the brush, she sees that the paint hanging from it is already completely dry and looks lumpy. Sighing, she throws the mascara into the small trash can under the sink. While her hair is drying, she makes herself a coffee and dresses after drinking it. She chooses an airy, colorful blouse and jeans she hasn't worn for ages. For quite a while, black or gray clothes seemed more appropriate to her. But that's over now! Jochen is right, she cannot wear mourning all her life.

A while later, after another coffee, she sets off for the city. Today she doesn't walk but goes directly to the nearest bus stop. She takes the bus past the places where she usually puts up her posters, past the barren property with the abandoned house, the sight of which often makes her melancholic and sad. She turns her head away as the bus approaches it, and by the time she looks through the large panorama window a few breaths later, they have already passed it. The opaque windows, nailed with slats, stare after the bus.

As they drive past the library, she feels a stinging pain in her chest. This is where her daughter was last seen alive.

# March 9, 2016

Shortly after Laura Wenz disappeared, the newspaper published a report about the missing child and called on the population to help. On the same day, a witness reported to the police – a librarian, who claimed to have seen the girl on the evening of her disappearance and to have observed something potentially significant. A comparison with the computer of the lending library where she worked confirmed this statement. Laura had borrowed a book there the day she disappeared.

Adelheid Stemmler put the investigators on to something. A few patrol cars were immediately sent off. Anton Wacholski was brought to the station to be questioned as a witness. In addition to the police officers of the criminal investigation department, police sergeant Likar, who had been the first to come into contact with the case, was also present during the interrogation. Even at a cursory glance he considered the witness suspicious. Which man just spent so much time in the library, reading to small children and calling himself 'Grandpa Anton'? Pedophiles often use such methods, join sports clubs, engage in charitable work for the supposed benefit of the children to approach their victims unnoticed. Grandpa Anton's leisure activities made him seem highly suspect.

A closer interrogation confirmed Likar's suspicion, as Wacholski quickly became entangled in his statements. At first he only admitted having seen the girl in the library. "Yes, I saw the little one. She was sitting next to me in one of the reading corners."

"Wasn't it rather the case that you sat down with her, Mr. Wacholski?" Likar asked. "And that you also started talking to the girl? What did you say to her?"

Wacholski, who had seemed quite calm at first, quickly became nervous. Unconsciously he blinked faster, his right foot bobbed restlessly up and down.

"Actually, I wasn't talking to her at all. I wanted to tell her something, but when I spoke to her, she immediately got up and left. That's all I can tell you. I don't know this girl at all."

"Did you frighten Laura with what you said?" came a suspicious interjection from one of the police officers.

"Listen, that's absurd. She just jumped up immediately because she didn't want to miss her bus. Are you insinuating that I have something to do with her disappearance?"

When Likar dug deeper why Wacholski knew so well that the girl was in a hurry, he became more and more nervous. His entire posture revealed his tension. The officials put pressure on him.

"There must have been a reason why the girl almost ran away after you had spoken to her. We have a witness statement that tells us exactly this scene. How can you explain this to us, Mr. Wacholski?"

Eventually Grandpa Anton floundered and contradicted his previous statement. Suddenly he talked about having seen her on her way home because she had missed her bus. He claimed that already in the library he had the impression that the girl was being watched and followed by a young man. Therefore, out of pure concern, he would have approached her and later offered to drive her home. His statement sounded confused and the strange man he had allegedly seen seemed to be a protective statement. A bungling attempt to turn the

62

suspicion away from himself. His description of the person also remained vague. In his mid-thirties or late twenties, hard to say, tall, muscular. Wacholski also couldn't remember the color of his hair.

"Black or brown, maybe blonde, but very dark," he said, adding that he didn't have a very good personal memory, but would certainly recognize him if he saw him. Wacholski talked himself into trouble. He quickly came into the focus of the investigation.

# April 12, 2017

After Laura's tracks could be traced to the library, the police also assumed a crime. Runaways didn't go to the library to borrow a book for their trip. Secretly, the officers were just waiting for her body to be found somewhere. The criminal investigation department was called in, as with any suspected capital crime. They had more experience in investigating smuggling gangs, traffickers of girls and the like. But in such cases, as Tatjana was told by one of the officials, it would usually be more the case that girls from the Eastern Bloc were abducted and forced into prostitution in the rich West. Such a thing would happen rather seldom the other way round.

Routine checks of potential suspects or correspondingly previously convicted persons followed. Nevertheless, the police found no indication of where Laura might have disappeared to. This guy Wacholski, who had last seen her, was the only clue. A search warrant was requested for his house and car in a hurry, while he was still being questioned as a witness at the precinct. The hope and urge to find the girl quickly was huge. So it was no surprise that they concentrated on the first suspect too willingly – and got bitterly disappointed.

Tatjana also threw herself in at Anton Wacholski in a fury and still feels terrible when she thinks of this poor man.

Fortunately, they quickly pass the library and approach the center of the small town. During the few minutes that the journey still takes, Tatjana tries to free herself from the thoughts of Laura and the investigations. She doesn't want to fall back into her sadness as if it was a big black hole with high attraction. That's why she looks at every border with blossoming spring flowers that they pass and reads the posters at an advertising pillar next to a traffic light at which they stop. She gets off at the bus station, walks through the city center and looks at the displays of the shops to which she has paid too little attention for too long. The colorful summer fashion, which is already on display everywhere, is really beautiful. Part of her old self, the woman she used to be, seems to have awakened again. She doesn't know why, but she tries to enjoy it.

She used to be enterprising, full of joie de vivre, had hobbies and friends. She had little in common with this sad old woman who has been looking at her from the mirror lately. Her friends, at first worried and by her side, had increasingly been distancing. Tatjana knows that she isn't entirely innocent of this, because her grief takes up so much space that there is less and less room for other people.

First, the already casual acquaintances disappeared. Tatjana didn't even blame them. She liked the embarrassing speechlessness, which resulted from the fact that there were simply no suitable or appropriate words, just as little as the pitiful phrases. Or, even worse, the words

64

of encouragement with which some tried to express their sympathy. She literally chased one of her oldest friends to hell after he expressed his regret as if Laura hadn't only disappeared, but was already dead.

In the meantime, not even her former best friend shows up very often anymore, because she also snubbed Jutta many times in the last year, which is why she has stopped her attempts to pull Tatjana out of her mental hole.

She's thinking about Jochen. She's aware that she also pushed him away more and more in the past year and she hopes that he will be positively surprised when tonight a woman awaits him who is a little more like the woman he married many years ago. He is right, she mustn't look back all the time. Hopefully he likes the change and it will elicit a smile and a compliment – maybe he will notice her again.

Tatjana enters the big drugstore market in the city's only and therefore largest shopping center and looks searchingly around. It takes her almost ten minutes to choose a mascara from the huge assortment. Then she stands undecided in front of the shelf with the hair colors. Which one should she take? More minutes pass and she is so focused on this question that she doesn't even notice that one of the employees is looking at her and has been watching her for a while. Finally he steps next to her, reaches into the shelf and pulls out a warm brown tone with a slight tinge of red.

"I think this color would look very good on you." He holds out the package to her. Surprised, Tatjana looks up at him and wonders. He looks vaguely familiar to her.

"Thank you," she replies timidly as she grasps and examines the color. Then she takes a closer look at the salesman. She has seen him before, he looks familiar to her – but where from?

"A beautiful shade," she thanks him and then asks, "Do we know each other from somewhere?"

A strange, slightly agonized expression scurries over his face and that's when the penny drops: The other day in the park! The man who for a moment seemed to want to say something. That was him!

# March 6, 2016

The girl in the basement started screaming and ended Tom's pondering. He heard her pointed, panicked screams, muffled by the door. It was about time she finally regained consciousness! A grin crept to his face as he stubbed out his cigarette on the floor. Then he stood up and went to the back door with the creaking hinges. He opened it a little, just enough to slip out, and walked around the house. In front of the basement windows he paused and listened.

Nothing could be heard except for the whistling of the wind and the motor of a passing car. His grin widened. Old egg cartons, carpets from the upper floors, half-rotten foam mattresses. With these and other materials he had insulated the outer walls of the cellar room, what had been a damn drudgery. Furthermore he had nailed thick wooden planks in front of the insulation and then tested the sound-absorbing effect with a radio turned to the highest volume. At the moment he just wanted to play it safe, do everything right, avoid beginners' mistakes. So he waited until the noise of the motor had faded away, listened hard and was satisfied that there was no sound outside.

Back in the house he went to the cellar door and listened as the sharp screams slowly turned into a desperate, frightened whimper. Purposefully, he walked through the kitchen into an adjoining room where he had placed the generator. From there a cable led down to the dungeon where it powered a naked light bulb on the ceiling. Powerfully he pulled on the starter. But the generator made nothing more than a stuttering noise and wouldn't start no matter how hard it pulled. He had probably forgotten to fill up the gasoline after using the generator last time. Neither had he thought of getting new gas. Angry with himself, he kicked against the empty canister, which clattering fell over.

"Fucking shit!"

He decided to check on the girl again shortly and come back the next day. From down below, the soft whimpering still came through the door. He unlocked it, turned on the flashlight and went down the stairs. As soon as his footsteps sounded, the girl was as quiet as a mouse. As if she wanted to hide from him; probably trying to pretend she wasn't there at all. The beam of light found the corner of the mattress. Tom's mood rose suddenly when he saw the object of his desire. She crouched at the outer edge of the mattress, her legs pulled close to her body, and she stared anxiously in his direction. He shone right in her face, which she hurriedly turned away blinded by the sudden brightness. Shielding, she held her outstretched hand towards him, blinking violently and trying to recognize the person behind the flashlight.

"Please, what do you want from me? Do you want money? My parents will pay what you want! But please, let me go! Please," the girl now began to beg in a tearful voice. With real fear resonating in it! Tom already felt something moving in his pants.

"Schhh," he hissed softly. "We'll get to that. Tomorrow. I have to do something first." He let the flashlight beam glide over the floor until he found the bucket Laura had knocked over when falling from the stairs. He picked it up and put it at the foot of the mattress.

"If you have to … you know," he informed her briefly before he turned away and went back to the stairs. When he reached the top, he shone back to Laura again.

"Sleep well!" he said. "Tomorrow I'll come to visit you and bring you some breakfast."

Laura's fear of being left alone in the dark again gained the upper hand and triumphed over her fear of her kidnapper: "Wait! Don't leave me here alone!" Her voice panicked. "At least leave me the flashlight! Please!" Instead of answering her, Tom just grinned and turned off the lamp, which turned her begging into an anxious squeaking. Laughing, he turned on the flashlight and dazzled her again. Then he left the cellar.

"At least tell me what you want from me!" she screamed after him. Tom grinned. She'd find out soon enough. He carefully locked the cellar door before taking the empty petrol canister and his cigarettes, which were still on the kitchen table, and leaving the house through the back door. The rusty hinges creaked like in agony.

*\*\*\**

While her kidnapper mounted the gasoline canister on his bicycle and made his way home, Laura palpated along the chain and crawled to the middle of the room. It had to be fastened somewhere on the ceiling, probably on a hook. Laura pulled the chain, jerked on it, hung herself on it with all her weight, but she couldn't release it. Minutes of effort brought nothing but despair. Finally she gave up and fumbled back to the mattress. Disoriented at first, she crawled in the wrong direction until she was stopped by the ankle shackle. She had never liked being in the dark and it was so gloomy here that she couldn't see anything at all. Laura turned around and crawled in the other direction until her head banged against a wall. Panic rose in her. She bravely fought against it and fumbled along the wall until she found her bed again.

After this futile attempt to free herself, Laura sat trembling in the corner and tried to calm down. She was terrified, but tried not to go crazy. The man had done nothing to her. Sure, there had been his blows when he captured her. But since then he had left her in peace, promised her breakfast, had put this bucket there for her and otherwise hadn't tried to do anything to her. Surely he was after money. Her parents weren't rich. Maybe he had confused her with another girl and would let her go if he noticed the mistake. Or he actually tried to blackmail her parents. This thought had a calming effect on her because she knew that her parents would do anything in their power to get her out of here. The kidnapper surely called her parents at that moment to demand the amount to be paid.

*My cell phone!* Shot through her head. *Mama said, you can always dial the emergency call, even without any credit!* Hope spread inside her and she hurriedly started to search her pockets. It was gone! She groped around in the dark until she found her Hello-Kitty-bag, which she no longer found stupid but clasped like a lifebelt. A familiar object in a cold, strange and threatening environment. She fumbled the clasp with her fingers up and down. Perhaps she had put the phone in her pocket? Or …? She rummaged through the bag, although she remembered exactly how she had the phone in her jeans, listened to music, and pulled the plug out of her ear when this lunatic appeared next to her. How could she be so stupid as to trust him?

70

She screamed as she stabbed herself in the index finger with the compass she had taken with her for geometry lessons. She stuck her finger in her mouth, sucked it. It tasted metallic, but quickly stopped bleeding. The finger probably swelled, for it pounded hellishly. A few tears rolled down her cheeks and she vigorously wiped them away. Laura reached into her pocket again, more carefully this time, and took out the compass. Her fist clenched around it, holding it like a weapon. She didn't know how hard it was to hurt someone with a compass. A knife would certainly be better. But nothing else was available. Maybe she could use it for defense when her kidnapper returned.

Laura trembled more and more. This was partly due to fear, but mainly to the fact that it was bitterly cold in her dungeon. She could not find a blanket. She tried to remember what little she had noticed when the man with the flashlight had been in the cellar. But there weren't any useful memories. Only the shadows she could see in the darkness behind the light and the pain that drilled into her brain when the blackness was suddenly followed by much too bright light falling directly in her eyes. Something to improve her present situation didn't occur to her either. So she moved her bag to the suspected head end of the mattress, hid her hand with her weapon underneath and put her head on it. Better than no pillow at all. And always better than putting your head on the musty smelling mattress, which was moldy and clammy under the cold rubbery cover. She rolled herself up as far as the ankle shackle would allow, pulled her sweatshirt over her tightened knees and hoped she would get a little warm. Eventually, after lying there freezing for an eternity, she felt less cold. Laura's body was at the end of its strength, the tiredness became overwhelming. Although she tried to stay awake so that she would hear the kidnapper return, she fell into a deep, exhausted sleep, from which she only woke with a start again when the cellar door opened noisily the next day.

# April 12, 2017

"You know who I am!" it bursts out of Tatjana. More determining than guessing. The man whose name tag identifies him as branch manager Oliver Nagel nods seriously and silently.

"Yeah, I know. You're the mother of this missing girl. Laura. I have often wondered whether it would be appropriate to contact you personally and express my condolences."

Tatjana looks at him in surprise. Why should he do that? Had he known her daughter?

"Then why did you run away from me in the park the other day? That was you, right? And why should you condole personally in the first place?"

Nagel starts to explain, "I'm sure you know that your daughter ordered some photos that were never picked up. When we found out who was in the pictures, we handed them over to the police. I'm sure the officers told you that."

Tatjana nods confirmingly.

"That's why I thought … It just seemed appropriate to me. I don't know what was going on with me in the park the other day. Your sadness was so obvious and as one of the last to see your daughter alive …"

One of the last? What does he want to tell her with these words? Tatjana's heart seems to stop for a moment before she asks tonelessly: "What are you trying to say? Do you know what happened to my daughter? Do you know where she is?" Her eyes are wide open; fear and the sudden hope of learning something new can be read from her facial expressions.

"I don't know where she is. But I was able to listen to the conversation she had with her friend on the day she disappeared."

Tatjana's eyes are widening even more. The officials hadn't told her about that. Her voice becomes louder and more demanding when she asks, "So you heard where she wanted to go?"

"No, not even that. But listen, we should go to my office and ..." Nagel says, but Tatjana won't let him finish. Her tone becomes more shrill because she can hardly bear the inner tension. Her voice now sounds interspersed with an unpleasant, slightly hysterical note: "Don't let me beg for every word! Tell me what you heard! Where is my Laura?"

The irrational hope that this man might know something about Laura's whereabouts makes her lose her mind for a moment. She's not thinking logically right now. It doesn't occur to her that the police would have followed up this clue long ago. The first heads of customers standing nearby are already turning to them.

"Listen, I don't know where ..."

"What have you heard? Now tell me what you know!" Now she's yelling at him. Even more heads turn to them.

"Calm down, please," soothes the manager and she actually shuts up. He grabs her gently but forcefully by the elbow and directs her to his office. He closes the door and is visibly relieved because they no longer attract everyone's attention. During the few meters that they have covered, Tatjana has regained some self-control, seems calmer again and now asks very composedly, "Well, what do you know about my child?"

"First of all," the man begins slowly, "I want to tell you how sorry I am for ..."

Again, he doesn't get far because Tatjana interrupts him. She doesn't want to hear phrases or pitiful words, she wants to know what he knows. Again she gets louder: "Shit, stop beating around the bush! Tell me what you know?"

He offers her a seat, sits behind his desk and tells her what he can remember. He tells her about the conversation between the girls, about which he had already told the investigating officers. He tries to find words for how concerned he is about this matter and emphasizes how often he had to think of Laura.

"You know, just before her daughter disappeared, my girlfriend had told me she's expecting a child. When I saw your daughter in our shop, such a delightful child, I thought maybe it wouldn't be so terrible to become a father. When I read in the newspaper that she didn't come home anymore ... For a few months now I have a little daughter of my own. Maybe that's why the disappearance of your Laura affected me so deeply. You see, that's my little one."

The store manager pushes a photo of his baby across his desk. Tatjana takes a quick look at it. The sight of the newborn in connection with her own loss is more than she can bear at the moment. Abruptly she gets up, turns her back on him. She hates to burst into tears in front of strangers, but she can't help it. They now run down her cheeks in rapids. She wipes her eyes with an energetic gesture. Meanwhile she' accustomed to suppressing her feelings and has quickly regained control. Just when she's about to turn back to Mr. Nagel, her gaze falls on something lying on top of a box in the shelf in front of which she is standing. She reaches out, grabs it and inspects the find. Suddenly she feels ice-cold. With the filigree necklace and the heart-shaped

75

pendant in her hand, she turns to Nagel and shows it to him.

"How did you get this?" she wants to know.

"This chain?" he asks in surprise. "Our cleaners found it under a shelf. A customer must have lost it while shopping."

"This necklace belonged to Laura!" She shows Nagel the detail that makes her so sure. "Look, there on the pendant, in the left corner of the heart, there's a little stone missing. It broke out the first day after I gave it to her. She jokingly bit it to see if the diamonds were real."

The branch manager examines the described position. "Unbelievable!" Nagel is amazed. Then a radiant smile brightens his face, "Then I am especially happy to finally be able to return this find. I guess there's no reason why you shouldn't take the necklace with you. The police probably won't be able to do much with it and already know that Laura was here at that time. It's probably only a small consolation, but now you've got at least one souvenir back after your loss."

Tatjana doesn't get upset as she usually does when someone talks about her loss like that.

"Perhaps Laura isn't lost, but only misplaced," she replies on better days. This time she refrains from any contradiction and doesn't inform the branch manager about the inner life of the pendant. She fears that he might insist on handing over the find to the police. It's difficult for her to find the right words to thank him for the gift he just gave her. She gets up, walks around the desk and takes him in her arms, this strange man who has given her something that no one could have expected: a piece of Laura that had been lost but found again. Then all of a sudden she's in a terrible hurry to say goodbye.

76

While leaving, she hardly pays attention to the way or the people who come towards her. She can hardly believe what has just happened to her and what she now holds in her hand. A gift from Laura. No sign of life, but after such a long time in which she had nothing but the hope that is ever harder to keep alive, this heart is almost as good. She can't wait to come home to sit at her computer and see what's stored on the chip inside of it.

She's so impatient that it's hard for her to sit still on the bus. Tatjana doesn't look out of the window, but stares at the heart, plays with it nervously and lets the necklace slide from hand to hand. She turns the heart back and forth, pulls the two halves apart, which are held together magnetically. She stares at the USB stick as if she could decipher its secrets with her penetrating gaze, without any technical aids.

"Fucking shit! Why don't you open your eyes when you're driving, you stupid idiot!"

The rude exclamation of the bus driver and the sharp braking of the vehicle wakes her from her thoughts. Tatjana sits in the front row of the bus and through its large windscreen she sees a cyclist swerving onto the street. His bike is heavily loaded with large gasoline canisters hanging on both sides of the luggage carrier. A glance to the side shows her that he came from the entrance of a gas station. Provocatively he slowly cycles in front of the bus, in the middle of the road. "Get out of the way!" the bus driver shouts. The bus rolls at a snail's pace behind the bike, and due to oncoming traffic, overtaking is out of the question. Behind them the horns are already honking. Slowly the rider's face gets covered with red spots of excitement. Tatjana says nothing, but inside she also curses. After all, she is in a hurry to get to her computer. A few crossroads further the cyclist finally turns off, and as he goes into the bend, she notices the paintwork on his bike. It's black with yellow and orange flames. *The same idiot who splashed me the other day. Too bad that the bus driver could still brake*, she thinks for a nasty moment. Then she remembers what a delay such an accident would have caused and is nevertheless glad that nothing has happened.

Finally at home, she immediately starts the computer, shoves the memory card into the designated slot with excitedly trembling fingers and breathlessly clicks through the pictures that open on the screen in front of her. There are so many! Laura in all her facets. She already knows some of the pictures, she made them herself when Laura was little. But there is also Laura in the park, Laura eating ice cream with her friends, Laura alone in front of the mirror in the bathroom and Laura full of life on a meadow, laughing and posing for the camera with a flower in her hair. One picture shows her before going to the cinema, outside in front of the film poster, another before she enters the cinema hall, with a large bag of popcorn in her hands. They had given her a digital camera last Christmas, and Laura had used it happily and often. Tatjana doesn't know many of the pictures yet. Each one of them is so wonderful in her eyes that its beauty cannot be surpassed. Tears are running down her cheeks, but she hardly notices that. She's so happy, but at the same time the longing for her child almost breaks her heart. Her tears aren't the only thing she doesn't notice at this moment. Later, when Jochen comes home, Tatjana runs towards him radiant with joy. She embraces him as soon as he closes the door behind him and presses a big kiss on his mouth.

"Wow, what's the matter with you? Did we win the lottery?" Jochen comments on the unexpectedly joyful

78

greeting. He feels clumsy in her arms and doesn't return the hug immediately. Instead of an answer, she gives him another kiss. Finally, he puts his arm around her hip. Tatjana would love to burst out with the great news immediately, but she wants to make it a bit exciting.

"I was in town today. You'll never guess what I brought with me," she stirs up his curiosity a little more and snuggles up to him.

His grip becomes a little tighter.

"I'm curious."

"Come on, guess!"

"You emptied a lingerie boutique and brought me something nice to unpack?" Jochen guesses.

Tatjana laughs, "No, much better. I told you, you'll never guess! Just come with me, I'll show you something." Tatjana loosens his hand, which is still on her hip, takes it and drags him with her. Jochen has to see it with his own eyes. She's so looking forward to his surprised, disbelieving look.

"It's nice to hear you laugh again," he says as he climbs up the stairs behind her. Tatjana leads him to her office.

"Have a seat, Mr. Wenz!" With an inviting gesture she points to the chair in front of her computer. He follows her request, sits and asks, "And what now? Shall I close my eyes?"

Tatjana laughs again. "On the contrary, open them wide!" Then she sits down on his lap, grabs the mouse and opens the folder with the pictures. With a few clicks she brings a slide show onto the screen. While one picture after the other appears on the monitor, she tries to put into words what has happened, and Jochen gets a confused summary of the events.

Tatjana chatters excitedly, her gaze sticking to the screen. Only when her explanations are finished does she look up, expecting a reaction from him. But Jochen remains mute and his facial expression is strange. Sad and desperate, no trace of joy. Finally he opens his mouth and only one question comes out, "Are there pictures on it that were taken after her disappearance?"

*After her disappearance.* Jochen can't even say her name. When Tatjana says no, he pushes her silently from his lap and stands up. His eyes fill with tears. He doesn't look at the photos again, turns around and leaves the room. Tatjana's joy also fades away suddenly. Dejected, she follows Jochen with her eyes and feels how the familiar feeling of hopelessness is once again spreading in her. She remains sitting for a moment as if she has turned into stone. His reaction makes her perplexed, angry, sad – she can't even define exactly what it triggers in her. Then she gets up and follows him.

She finds Jochen in Laura's room, sitting on her bed. He has his head buried in his hands and looks up as he hears her enter. She has never seen him looking so desperate, not even when the fear for Laura was still fresh. And even before he opens his mouth, she knows that she doesn't want to hear what he has to say. She can read it in his eyes and defensive posture when she wants to go to him and take him in her arms.

"Don't!" he fends her off. A moment of silence follows before he shakes his head – not to deny something, but to emphasize his words.

"Tatjana, I can't take any more!" With this one sentence he actually already says everything and she hears how the blood begins to roar in her ears while he continues, "I'm sorry. You know I love you. I really love you. But I can't go on living like this anymore!"

80

Tatjana's legs suddenly feel as if they were made of rubber and couldn't carry her any further. While a world collapses inside her, she lets herself sink powerlessly onto the carpet in front of Laura's bed. Jochen is her family – everything that's left of it. She can't imagine a life without him! She would love to plead, "Don't go!" But she doesn't, because she knows it would be pointless. Never in all those years, not even in an argument did Jochen threaten to leave her. Now he's said it openly. Tatjana knows that he has made his decision. That's why she says in a quiet, almost toneless voice, "If that's the case, then get out of here!"

She remains sitting while Jochen walks over into the bedroom.

A quarter of an hour later she's still sitting there.

"Tatjana." Jochen is standing with a packed bag in the door frame. She looks up at him with a petrified face and doesn't say a word.

He stammers helplessly, "Please give me a few days. Don't call me, please! I need to find some distance and clear my head. Maybe I'll have enough strength again when I get some rest. It's probably best if I first move into a hotel. I really can't take any more, but I promise you, I'll call you and we can talk about everything when I've got a little strength."

Tatjana remains silent. She just nods. Jochen waits a moment before he grabs his bag a little tighter and turns around. Only when she hears the front door closing, her inner and outer rigidity dissolves. She trembles uncontrollably, and as her tears start to flow, she crawls over to Laura's bed, on which she cries until she falls asleep completely empty and exhausted.

# March 7, 2016

Statistically speaking, it's not uncommon that perpetrators have been victims themselves—mostly in their childhood—and that they pass on their own humiliation in a kind of forced repetition.

Such statistics didn't interest him. Such a psycho shit didn't apply to him. Tom had simply realized early on that he enjoyed it and that he even felt lust when others suffered and submitted to him – when he was the boss. It started with small things like trying to roast an ant with the help of the sun and a magnifying glass. With forcing a smaller boy to eat a nudibranch to amuse the others he was playing with. With the feeling of power that went with it.

But Tom had improved pretty quickly. He was eight when he took care of the fish in his father's aquarium. His dad loved his guppies and neons. On weekends he often spent hours changing the water, cleaning the pump and vacuuming the gravel. Tom found his hobby very boring. His first attack on the fish was to beat up another boy to take away his pocket money. With that money he bought a full-grown scalar in the nearby pet shop, which he put in the aquarium while his father was at work. He spent the rest of the afternoon in front of this small wet world and watched the predator fish hunting the small ornamental fish. Successfully! Soon he had eaten a good part of them. Tom later told his horrified father that he had only wanted to please him with the big fish. His father was so touched that he didn't have the heart to just fish out the gift and bring it back to the pet shop. So he left the scalar in the pool. Within a few weeks there were only the fastest and largest guppies left who had managed to hide quickly enough between the leaves of the aquatic plants as soon as the triangular predator came swimming. One afternoon, when he was almost bored to death, Tom took two packs of salt from the pantry and poured them into the water. The effect was devastating.

"I just wanted the fish to have it nice!" he said in the evening. "Like in the sea. The water is also salty there. I only made them sea water!" Besides he squeezed a few tears out of his eyes, and they didn't miss their effect. The fish had all died, but his father forgave him – believing Tom hadn't intended anything bad. However, he gave up his hobby and mothballed the aquarium.

Tom's next victim was Fredi the hamster. A mouse-trap placed in the cage broke his neck. Nevertheless, Fredi had still squeaked and beeped a little before he was dead. When he told his father in the evening that Fredi had accidentally fallen, his father probably suspected for the first time that Tom wasn't telling the truth. He gave him an unusually long lecture on the great responsibility of having a pet and the obligation to treat it well.

Tom, however, found it fascinating to watch others suffer – no matter if they were humans or animals. To be in control of who lives and who dies – or who stretches out their tongue to lick out the bowl in the school toilet and who doesn't.

Of course, his sadistic tendencies had been noticed from time to time during his adolescence. His mother even dragged him to the psychiatrist after the incident with the damn cat of the neighbor. But when the psychiatrist sought the blame more in his parents than in him and even suspected abuse, the visits to the shrink quickly stopped. What this idiot hadn't figured out was that he didn't do such things to cope with any bad experiences, but because it gave him pleasure.

Very early in his life, Tom himself experienced the cellar where he had locked Laura up. If Tom had done something really bad and a telling-off was not enough, his father locked him up down there as a punishment. Alternatively, he offered to spank him briefly and painfully. He let Tom choose which punishment he wanted, the painful one or the longer one. Tom usually decided on the cellar. There he should think about what he had done wrong. Normally the door opened again after not too long. Rarely did he have to stay there longer than an hour. And when he then apologized for his behavior and promised to make more effort in the future, then he was allowed to come back up again. In truth, the cellar was no punishment at all for Tom. He spent his time down there catching daddy-long-legs and spiders to rip their legs out and skewer woodlice on small sticks. He called it 'cellar shashlik'. Once he smuggled a skewer outside, and a boy who was new in the neighborhood had to gnaw it off.

"Listen, this is my gang! Either you eat the cellar shashlik now or you can leave right away. Then you mustn't join in," he had put the newcomer under pressure. Tom was in charge of his clique, which included most of the boys in the neighborhood. "Close your eyes and do it!" The new guy had been on the verge of crying, had looked around in bewilderment – looking for at least someone to return his gaze and stand by him. Tom was no taller or stronger than his friends back then, but he was more unrestrained, brutal, and willing to get his way by manipulating them. On the one hand, grossly by violence, but also in another, almost more effective way:

He gave them the choice of which side they were on. On the enemy side or on his. Hardly anybody wanted to stand up to Tom. The only one who didn't immediately look away or down on the ground was a slim boy. But instead of the help he had hoped for, the new boy only got one good piece of advice: "Just do it! Tom will force you to eat the shashlik anyway. If you don't do it voluntarily, he won't let you join the gang. I'm sure it's not that bad. I had to eat a nudibranch. So, do it!" Then they had watched the new guy gnaw the skewer off and vomit afterward.

Tom was twelve and his sadistic tendencies were already clearly present when his old man caught him torturing his neighbor's cat in the shed next to the house. Tom had put the animal in a sack and poked the agonizingly meowing creature with a pointed stick. At one point a little blood was already pouring out and he found it great to watch the dancing sack in which the stupid thing made panicked but futile attempts to escape. He had been interested to know how long it would take for the cat to realize the hopelessness of the situation and to accept its fate. Unfortunately, he had no chance to complete his experiment. Ten minutes of real fun and the first erection of his life hadn't been enough. His father caught him and beat him all the way back into the house. Inside he locked Tom up in the basement, where he let him stay in the dark for hours this time. When the old man came back, he was drunk as a skunk – and then he used the tip of his cigarette.

"You like that?" the old man had asked him with a grin while he held him by his neck and pressed the hot embers on his defenseless skin until a screeching scream of pain escaped him. The answer was: Yes, he liked such things. He just didn't feel like being a victim in such a scenario. But Tom clenched his teeth instead of yelling his true feelings at the old man.

The next day, his father had apologized to him. He was ashamed of the fact that he had lost his self-control. After that Tom had the feeling that the old man would look at him differently. Disgusted, although or perhaps just because he wasn't any better himself, as he had proven down in the cellar. And also somehow afraid, as if he could now discover something in the boy that was dangerous, disgusting and evil. Something to beware of.

Until the incident with the cat, the old man had never touched him. Okay, a slap in the face now and then, a slap on the butt, a little stay in the cellar. Which boy doesn't need a strict hand? But he had never done more until that day, and even after that he never lost his self-control again. His father was a bourgeois who demanded that the food had to be on the table on time when he got home from work. Every Saturday he washed his car and cut the lawn regularly so the neighbors wouldn't get a bad impression. A righteous, simple citizen with solid values and morals, who actually didn't want to see how different his offspring had become. He was a man who abhorred violence of any kind and could give moral lectures for hours. And his mother – she, too, seemed blind to the dark side of her son. She believed his excuses far too willingly so that she wouldn't have to stop pretending to live in a perfect world. In the end, the assholes weren't interested in what was really going on anyway. As long as he didn't act stupid, but seemed remorseful and insightful when he was caught, everyone was happy. Most of the time he had a plausible reason, a halfway credible and conclusive story about what happened how and why, so he could hide his true nature. And, if necessary, he had an intimidated accomplice who was willing to testify to Tom's innocence. Actually, Tom had a great childhood. He lacked nothing. His parents did all they could to give him a good life and educate him to be a good person. Moped driver's license at the age of fifteen, always enough pocket money ...

Nevertheless, Tom was happy when he finally came of age and was able to leave the house. Already as a teenager he lifted dumbbells, did a lot of sports and had a high degree of self-control.

When he was eighteen, he took a job and financed a small apartment with the money he earned as a merciless trainer in a gym. On the weekends in summer, he also did black labor at the construction site. He rarely showed up at home. His self-control only suffered when it came to his somewhat out of the ordinary needs. His irresistible urge to torture and humiliate others. Sometimes he just went over the top. His last girlfriend had even threatened him with criminal charges because a passionate pat on the butt became a few more, while he had his way with her. The stupid bitch.

"You sick asshole! I should report you!" she had yelled while she hurriedly got into her clothes. When she wanted to run out of the apartment crying, he had held her tight, dug his thumb into one cheek and his other fingers into the other, held her weeping face like a vice and forced her to look up at him. He had stared straight into her eyes and threatened, "If you are so stupid as to turn me in, I'll show you what I am capable of! No matter where you go, I'll find you. And compared the what I'll do with you then, this was nothing at all!"

The look on her face told him she believed every word he said. Letting the bitch leave had taken him a lot of effort. His erection was enormous as he pressed her against the wall next to the apartment door and made her realize how stupid it would be to mess with him. Her crying fearful look and the feeling of power turned him on. It had been stimulating. He would have loved to have another round with her, but instead he had increased the pressure of his fingers, "Even if I had to go to jail, I'd find you, fuck you and drown you like a cat!" When he was halfway sure he had intimidated her enough, he pushed her out the door.

At first as an angry, frustrated thought, hateful while staring after the bitch, he had for the first time had the idea to have his own slut – one that he wouldn't have to let go. One from which no traces led back to him, and with whom he could do what he wanted. A possession – kept in a place where no one would look for it. But where to find such a place? Or a suitable victim?

For a while it remained an abstract thought to which he sometimes jerked himself off. Then something happened that shuffled the cards anew, created an opportunity and provided even more financial independence: his mother died. For the last few years she had lived alone in the house of his childhood. Meanwhile, his father lived in a nursing home where his mother had him permanently hospitalized after a severe stroke because it was beyond her strength to care for him at home. As far as he knew, she had visited him almost daily. Tom had visited him only once in the three years of the old man's stay there. For ages he had had very little contact with his parents. Although he lived only a few crossroads away from them, he hardly showed up there. Only by a call from their lawyer, Tom had learned of his loss, which he didn't feel to be one. The lawyer had condoled – and then he had asked him if he was ready to accept his inheritance.

He was more than ready! He had bought gasoline and dragged several canisters of it into the house – past the graves of Fredi the hamster and the neighbor's cat, on which there were still the old weathered crosses. Maybe they were the reason why he suddenly had to think of these old stories. More than ready, he now sat in the kitchen, which was part of his inheritance, smoking one last cigarette before starting the generator and taking a look at the cellar. And while grinding out his cigarette with the heel of his boot later, he decided to visit the old man.

# April 17, 2017

It's been five days since Jochen has left her. Since then Tatjana has hardly left the bed and hasn't looked at Laura's pictures either, because it would cause her too much pain. Jochen hasn't yet contacted her again. Actually, she had expected him to contact her at the latest after two or three days, a quiet weekend to clear his head. Five days seem far too long to her and she worries now. Tatjana doesn't even know where he is. He said he would go to a hotel. A few times she picked up the phone and was about to call him herself. But his urgent request to give him time kept her from doing so after all. In the last few days she had wept a lot, pitied herself and mourned her once perfect world, which is now completely in ruins. Several times she asked herself why she should still live now, after she has lost everything important to her. But a spark of hope remains. Maybe Jochen really only needs a few days for himself before he comes back to her.

Today, on the fifth day, she gets up at least, doesn't only go to the toilet, but also to the bathroom to take a hot shower. The water doesn't wash away her worries, but it revives her spirits at least partially. Then she hungrily plunders the fridge, because her appetite also suffered from the situation. While Tatjana sits in the kitchen and eats, she looks at the calendar hanging on the wall. A promotional gift from the pharmacy. It's attached to the hook where Laura's homemade annual calendars used to hang, which she brought back from kindergarten or school.

Today is Wednesday. On Wednesdays she goes to hang up her posters, most of which disappear without a trace just a few days later. She doesn't know who is tearing them down again and again, she hasn't seen anyone do it yet. But Tatjana doesn't get tired of hanging them up again and again. *Maybe*, she thinks, *this search is all I have left!* She won't give up. Today she will continue to search until she finds Laura. She decides that she will also fight for her husband. First she will put up her search posters, then she will buy the hair color she already had in her hand at the drugstore. She might even find some nice lingerie to give Jochen the surprise he had hoped for. Looking back, she wishes so much that she could turn back time and drag Jochen not into the office, but into the bedroom and get closer to her husband instead of losing him. Maybe it's not too late yet. She will set a sign with her transformation. And if he doesn't get in touch soon, then she will look for him, too.

Tatjana goes into the garage where they keep the tools and gets a hammer and nails. She always leaves the hammer on the chest of drawers next to the door. Jochen puts it back in the toolbox every week as if she wouldn't need it again soon. In the garage she thinks that maybe she can't have both. Her search and a life with Jochen. Tatjana isn't sure what she will decide for if Jochen should actually give her a choice.

A little later Tatjana walks her usual way, hangs up the first poster at the bus stop in her street, goes past the playground and the kiosk, then past the empty factory and the abandoned house, with the usual feeling of inner emptiness. Today she doesn't feel like making up stories about it. She gets on the bus, drives past the library, where she isn't allowed to hang up her posters. At the beginning that wasn't a problem, but after the thing with Grandpa Anton …

Tatjana feels a lump in her throat when she thinks of him. She also has a hard time dealing with this part of the story.

SUSPECT IN THE LAURA CASE IN INVESTIGATIVE CUSTODY the newspapers proclaimed a few days after the assumed crime. *Police arrested 53-year-old Anton W., who had retired early, based on a testimony. The 34-year-old librarian Adelheid S. was able to observe how the urgently suspected man approached the girl on the afternoon the thirteen-year-old Laura W. disappeared. "Laura seemed to be afraid of him and ran away when he approached her," Adelheid S. told the police. The investigation is still ongoing.*

Of course, Anton Wacholski was under suspicion after such a statement. The way he got entangled in his own words during the interrogation also made him appear suspect. At first he only said that he had seen the girl in the library. But then, when he was describing another man whom he thought was observing the girl, a fatal sentence slipped out of his mouth. The effort to dramatize the degree of his concern, to direct suspicion towards an unknown third person, broke his neck in interrogation. He had suddenly testified that he had offered Laura to bring her home so that nothing would happen to her because he didn't trust this other guy. And he assured that he didn't want to hurt the girl after all. The officials hadn't missed the meaning of his words. The library was probably not the last place he had seen Laura. After his testimony, Wacholski was not allowed to walk again. On urgent suspicion he was taken directly into pretrial custody.

His neighbors, his family, everybody learned what Wacholski was accused of. And of course Tatjana; she was even present at the arrest.

"We have a suspect. We'll pick him up now and take him to the precinct. With a bit of luck you'll soon have your daughter back," one of the policemen who had just rummaged through her own house told her, and hurriedly got into their official cars.

Tatjana didn't hesitate and just followed the policemen. She had seen him being led out of the house while the neighbors curiously came outside to find out why several emergency vehicles were parked in their street. Some of them shrouded their curiosity by secretly peering out from behind the curtains. For a moment Tatjana remained behind the wheel of her car, undecided what to do next. Then Wacholski came into sight and she got out of the car completely out of her mind with fear for her child. She is still ashamed of what followed. Seeing the alleged offender in front of her, even without knowing what exactly he had done or if he had done anything at all, triggered too much in her.

The anger and fear that she had been controlling as well as she could for days now broke out of her. Like a fury, she threw herself at the man, beat him, punched him with her fists, and it took three officers to pull her away from him. Nevertheless, she managed to spit hatefully in his face beforehand.

His alibi for the evening of Laura's disappearance finally proved to be airtight. There weren't any traces of Laura, neither in his house nor in his car. The trail which seemed so promising at first led to nowhere. They had to let Wacholski go. But his reputation was damaged forever. He was asked not to come to the library anymore. Some parents had expressed concerns and threatened not to allow their children to visit the library if he continued to hang out there. Otherwise Tatjana did not know much about this man. Maybe he had had other, bigger problems, but she was shocked and felt strangely guilty when Anton Wacholski committed suicide a few weeks later.

Then Tatjana was asked not to place her posters in the library anymore.

"You know, it's not good publicity that the girl was last seen here," the librarian explained in an apologetic tone. "And the parents already are worried enough. Please understand that you can no longer post your search notices here." Tatjana saw how unpleasant this conversation was for her. But something else could be read in Mrs. Stemmler's facial expressions: the tormenting feeling of guilt.

Finally the bus reaches its terminus. Tatjana gets off at the bus station, equips several lantern poles with posters on her way to the park and nails her remaining copies to the trees there. Then, after careful consideration, sitting on a park bench under a weeping willow, she returns to the drugstore market. Determined, she picks her favorite color from the shelf and walks straight to the checkout. There she pays hastily – hoping not to cross the path of the salesman she's met the other day, because she doesn't want to think about this encounter anymore. Then she takes the next bus home.

At home Tatjana sees that the answering machine's message signal flashes. Her heart beats faster as she presses the button to listen. Maybe Jochen has finally called in. The tape presents her with a few moments of silence before a crackling sound tells her that the caller hung up without saying anything. "You have no further messages," the device informs her afterward.

*Maybe he'll call tonight,* she thinks hopefully and swallows her disappointment. Maybe he tried it earlier, but didn't want to talk to the tape. Tatjana knows that Jochen doesn't like answering machines very much. Then she goes into the bathroom and spends almost an hour dyeing her graying hair. Such a little bit of color makes a grave visual difference. Before her eyes the haggard, sad woman she saw in the mirror disappears. A person appears she hasn't seen for a long time. She notices that this change is also good for herself – regardless of whether Jochen likes it or not. After she's finished, she feels fresher, stronger, as if she had changed more than just her hairstyle.

# March 7, 2016

The light bulb on the ceiling bathed the darkened room in a cold light, in which the girl sat shivering and full of fear. Laura's eyes ached and she blinked into the sudden brightness; suddenly torn from the exhausted twilight sleep into which she had fled. On the one hand she was glad not to be trapped in absolute darkness anymore, on the other hand she was scared of what the light would reveal.

Slowly her eyes got used to the new lighting conditions and now she could look around for the first time. The room she was in wasn't big, but spacious. Gray concrete floor, unadorned bare walls, two of them covered with roughly trimmed planks, a naked light bulb on the ceiling. A little beside it, an iron chain hung down and led to the shackle with which she was tied. In one of the corners stood a lonely chair. The mattress she was sitting on was wrapped in a black latex cover, next to her stood the still unused bucket. Her bladder now ached, but her shame kept her from relieving herself. As she correctly assumed, the light meant that she was about to have a visitor.

Her heart began to beat faster and seemed to jump out of her chest in fear as she heard the door to her dungeon being unlocked. Panically, she reached for the compass she had fished out of her pocket in the dark and held the pathetic weapon firmly. She pulled her legs tight to her chest and held her hand with the compass in between, so he wouldn't see it immediately. The sound of heavy boots rumbling down the stairs intensified the budding panic. Fearful, Laura raised her eyes as the steps stopped.

***

From wide-open eyes she stared at Tom and already in this moment he began to draw his satisfaction from the act.

Yes, he had the power and finally—for the first time in his life—he could act it out without having to fear unpleasant consequences. He squatted in front of her mattress and went to eye level. He reached out, which made her shrink back from at first. Therefore, he laughed briefly and gently stroked a strand of hair hanging from her teary face behind her ear.

"Did you sleep well, sweetheart?" Laura remained silent. Tom stayed calm and friendly and gently asked a second question, which he immediately answered himself, "Are you hungry? You must be hungry!"

Again she didn't answer, so he punched her in the face with her hand. He used his strength in a balanced way. His blow was firm and made her head fly to the side, but it wasn't so strong that she banged against the wall.

"I asked you a question," he rebuked her quietly, delighted at how she flinched with fear and perhaps a little pain, huddled together even more and began to stammer, "Y-yes, a little."

Again, he raised his hand and punched her on the other cheek. Then he stood up, looked down at her and said coldly, "That's 'Yes, master!'" Insecure, she looked up at him with tears in her eyes. Then Tom's face distorted. "Don't look at me like that, I was only kidding," he said with a broad grin. "You can simply call me Tom, we're friends after all."

Tom got up and went to the backpack he had left by the stairs and unpacked the breakfast he had brought with him. A bit away from her mattress, he placed the goods on the floor.

"Have you been to the toilet already?" he asked casually. He opened the mineral water bottle and slowly and leisurely filled a glass for her before taking care of the food. The rippling sound of the water reminded Laura of her aching bladder again and now it took all her willpower to keep it inside. Did he do it on purpose because he guessed how badly she needed to pee? she distorted her face in torment. He stood with his back to her so that she couldn't see exactly what he was doing, but he didn't stand in the way of her hearing. The splashing made it almost impossible for her to keep pulling herself together. But she made it. Finally the background noise changed from splashing to rattling. After a felt eternity, Tom seemed to be done with whatever he was doing, turned to her and presented her the breakfast. Suddenly Laura forgot every thought about the toilet. A mean grin crept over Tom's face as he saw her amazed gaze falling on the two freshly filled feeding bowls.

"Won't you come eat?" Laura shook her head vehemently. Absolutely not!

"I guess I have to motivate you a bit," Tom said, approaching Laura and squatting in front of her again. Laura took all her courage, pulled out her hand between her thighs as quick as a flash and rammed the compass down his throat with all her might. Tom screamed, surprised and in pain as his hand groped for his neck. He found the cold metal stuck in it. Without thinking about it, Tom put his hand around it and pulled it out. Almost in disbelief, he stared at the blood-stained compass now lying in his hand.

Fortunately, the thing had only hit his strong neck muscle and not his carotid artery.

"Shit! Have you gone completely crazy?" he yelled at Laura and threw the compass into a corner of the room that she couldn't reach due to her chain.

"You're a pretty pugnacious little beast! Is that allowed?" Now Tom was really angry. The wound on his neck quickly stopped bleeding, but she had irritated him with her fly bite. It was time to explain the rules of the house to her!

\*\*\*

It didn't take too long for Laura to lose the rest of her self-control. Tom had caught her like an animal, now he treated her as if she were nothing more than that. Her fighting spirit and her initial resistance quickly faded. As he approached her with clenched fists, she pissed her pants in fear. Protectively she pulled her arms up and her hands in front of her face. His beating fists knew no mercy.

Laura crouched in front of Tom on the dirty concrete floor. Her face was smeared with tears and the unappetizing food she had to eat from the bowl. She fought against a strong gag reflex and had to control herself not to vomit. Her body trembled uncontrollably with cold, but even more with fear. Tom patted her head patronizingly.

"Well done. Good girl! But look at you. You're all dirty." Tom reached into his pocket and pulled out a pocket knife, flipped out the blade, grabbed a strand of her hair and cut it off to show her how sharp the blade was.

"Come on, get up!" he said. Laura laboriously straightened herself up. She didn't dare to defend herself when Tom used his knife to cut up her favorite sweatshirt. She stood naked in front of him. She was still wearing her wet pants, and although she felt terribly cold in them, she almost couldn't bring herself to follow his next instruction.

"Take off your pants!" The fear of what he would do to her once she was completely naked was balanced by the fear of what would happen if she didn't obey his order.

"Do I have to help you along?" The quietly hissed question and his threateningly raised hand made her decide quickly. She unbuttoned her jeans with trembling fingers. Together with her also soaked underpants Laura pushed the jeans down. She tried to get out of the wet garment, but the ankle shackle made it impossible. She wriggled out of the jeans as far as she could, then Tom used the knife again. A few cuts later the soaked fabric lay in shreds at her feet.

Slowly Tom closed the knife again. Instead of putting it back in his pocket, he went over to the stairs and put it on the steps.

"Not that you'll get the idea of stealing from me and stabbing me while I'm busy with you," he commented on his action.

"And now let me have a look at you!" Grinning, he inspected her from head to toe. Laura instinctively raised her arms and tried to cover her most intimate parts with her hands.

"Don't!" he stopped her strictly. "Show yourself! Spread your legs a bit!" Hesitantly and deeply ashamed she obeyed.

"Now turn around. Show me your little ass," he continued. Laura felt so ashamed that she wished to ground would open and swallow her up. Tom examined her extensively, took his time. "Stay there," he ordered, then went to the mattress and took the bucket. Although it was unused and empty, he left the cellar with it.

Laura's gaze was stuck to the knife. Tom had given her a clear order and she was afraid of his reaction if she messed up what she was about to do. The fear of what he would do to her if she didn't manage to free herself quickly had grown immeasurably during the last minutes, eliminating her concerns. She just had to risk it!

Laura ran off, quickly mastered the few meters to the stairs – and was slowed down by her ankle shackle. With a painful scream she fell, stretched out her hands to catch the fall, but landed roughly on the ground. Her palms were burning. She had scraped them on the concrete floor.

A little motion made new pain shoot through her right wrist. She must have sprained it on impact. Laura tried to ignore the pain and reached for the knife. The attempt was doomed to failure – it was hopeless. No matter how much she stretched, she couldn't reach the knife. It was a small but crucial bit out of reach of what the restraints were granting her.

A thin desperate sound escaped her throat. Now she heard his footsteps approaching quickly. She panicked but couldn't get back to her place fast enough. She had almost arrived at the place when he had already reached the bottom of the stairs. She stared at him in shock.

"Didn't I tell you to stay where you were? Did you little bitch try to get the knife?" Tom asked sternly. His hand held the bucket he had filled to the brim with water.

"I'll have to teach you obedience."

Tom put the bucket next to her, bent down and picked up a shred of her cut-up sweatshirt. He pressed the piece of cloth into her hand and told her to wash herself.

The water was freezing cold. Nevertheless, Laura followed his command. She found it incredibly humiliating to clean herself in front of his eyes. The cold water made her tremble even more than she did because of the cold and fear. She obeyed without objection – despite everything she was happy to rinse the dog food and urine off her skin. When she had finished cleaning herself, Tom took the bucket and dumped the rest of the water over her. Panting, Laura gasped for air.

"Don't be such a pussy. It's just a little water," he commented with a grin.

Laura began to sob without restraint. "Why are you doing this? Why do you do that to me? Please, let me go!"

"No, Fida, I'm afraid I can't do that. You understand that. We're just getting to know each other a little better," he said to her and of course didn't even think about letting her go. He had completely different plans with her.

*Fida?* Hope grew in Laura. "My name ain't Fida. You have mistaken me for someone else! Please, just let me go, I won't tell anyone. I promise!"

Tom ignored her begging. He went over to the corner and got the chair, pulled it into the middle of the room

102

and sat down. Then he patted the side of his thigh with his hand before pointing to the floor next to him and saying with a cold smile, "Come here! Heel, Fida!"

At that moment Laura realized that he would never let her go again and all her hopes for a quick end to ransom blackmail died. The beating wasn't the worst. The most horrible moment hadn't been when she wet herself, nor when he'd forced her to crawl over the floor and eat from the bowls. Not the shame of washing in front of him or the rape that followed shortly afterward. The most horrible thing was this one moment when she realized that he was not in the least concerned about money and that her parents would never receive a ransom note – and that he would neither kill her nor release her.

When he was done with her, he rummaged again in his backpack and brought to light a long nightgown that he threw at her. "Here, you can put this on," he let her know before he left her alone. A few minutes after she heard him close the cellar door, the light bulb went out. The darkness took Laura firmly in its arms.

# March 7, 2016

That same afternoon, Tom visited his father in the nursing home. Only for the second time since his mother's death. The old man was still asleep when Tom entered his room and sat on a chair next to his bed. Tom wondered if he should just wake him up, but decided to wait a little until the old man came to. His face when he saw who was sitting by his bed was surely priceless!

While waiting, his brain played back the scenes he had just experienced again and again in his mental cinema, for him reviewing the whole thing with relish. It wasn't only as good as he had imagined, but it was BETTER. The sense of power he had felt when he descended into the basement was absolute and perfect. Intoxicating! Down there he was God. The excitement that went with it was unimaginable! Already the foreplay, the feeding, had got him excited. For the first time his real experiences matched his fantasies and ideas. What he imagined to be an ideal relationship was just beginning for Tom: To take ownership of Laura, to make her his willing possession, to discipline her until she wouldn't only accept her position in the relationship, but would even love it. Yes, that was his goal. In the end, he would control her completely, her body and her mind. She would belong to him alone! Like a faithful dog obeying his master's command.

How bewildered she had looked when she heard her new name and when he explained its meaning to her! Tom smiled at the memory. The name Fida was Arabic and meant 'devotion' and 'sacrifice'. It seemed to Tom more than suitable for the young bitch he would train.

The old man in the bed gave off a wheezing snore. Tom looked at him with contempt. The memory of his endless moral lectures revived in him. What would the old man have to say to his new pet? This memory also made him aware of the fact that he should treat his precious possession with care if he wanted to enjoy it for a long time.

Tom hadn't failed to notice how chilly it was down there in the basement. When he dropped his pants, he first thought his balls would freeze off. No shit! But he had warmed up quickly – as well as the little bitch, of course. At first she was quite stubborn, but he had taught her the ins and outs. That was so hot! Nevertheless he had to come up with something quickly, otherwise she would surely get ill down there. Maybe he would visit her again tonight and bring her a blanket. Couldn't do any harm. He didn't care if she froze or not, but she shouldn't get sick after all.

His Fida reminded him of the neighbor's cat that he had put in the sack as a child. It also didn't gain trust so quickly and didn't let itself get caught easily. Perhaps the animal felt that he was up to no good when he approached it with the sack. When he made the first attempt to catch it, it had hidden in a thorny bush. He had then spent half the afternoon patiently crouching in front of the bush, friendly speaking to the cat and luring it until it finally gave up its skepticism and cover. Grabbing it then, as it walked trustingly purring around his legs, had been child's play. You just had to have enough patience. Laura was like the cat: full of suspicion and justified distrust. But he didn't have to lure her and it didn't take hours of patience to catch her. He already had her in his sack, now it was time to let her dance.

After she hadn't moved immediately when he ordered her to heel, he had got up, had given her a loud slap in the face, had sat on the chair and given the command again. Only after the third repetition had she finally moved.

"You didn't do that correctly. Go back and do it again!" Without understanding Fida had stared at him, whereupon he got up, grabbed her by the neck and dragged her back to the place where she had stood before, and forced her on all fours, "Do it like a good doggie!" Only then the stupid slut had understood that she had to crawl in front of him. When Fida crawled towards him, his excitement had increased even more. Tom had felt the need to give his balls a little more room and slowly unbuttoned his pants. Only then had he noticed the cold.

"Are you still a virgin?" he wanted to know about her with a voice that was already rough with excitement, when he gave her the order to lie down on the mattress. A shy nod, paired with a fearful look from expectantly opened eyes, had been enough of an answer for him. At that moment he had a great idea. He had sat with her on the mattress and gently stroked a strand of her still wet hair from her face.

"Are you afraid I'll take your virginity by force?" The answer was easy to read in her face. Again she had nodded anxiously.

Like a cat that plays a little with a caught mouse before the deadly neck bite, he also wanted to prolong his pleasure a little. To increase it even more. That's why he had made her a promise, "You don't have to be afraid of that. I won't touch your little pussy until you ask me to. I promise."

Disbelieving relief and disgust were reflected in her facial expressions when she exclaimed with a thin voice, "I will never do that! Definitely not!"

Probably she had had to summon up all her courage for this one sentence. That amused him, which is why he contradicted with a grin, "Oh yes, Fida. You will! And until then I'll only fuck you in your little ass!"

Then he had ordered her to turn around and spread her buttocks a little for him. Again he had had to give some emphasis to his demand, but then she knelt before him and …

A suffocated noise ripped him from his thoughts. Tom looked up and saw the old man staring at him with his eyes wide open.

***

He must have fallen asleep after being fed his lunch by the pretty young thing that did a voluntary social year here. Wolfgang Richter blinked a few times, fought his way slowly up from the depths of sleep as he saw someone from the corner of his eye. A shadowy figure at the edge of his field of vision. He moved his head as far as he could still turn it to see who was sitting by his bed. A choked terrible sound escaped his otherwise speechless throat as he recognized the visitor. The boy had only been with him twice since his stroke, which sentenced him to life imprisonment in full mind in a paralyzed body that was barely functional. Wolfgang didn't like the memory of these visits.

"Hello, dad. Did you sleep well?" Thomas started the monologue.

"Well, what else can you do?"

Yes, that's how Wolfgang knew the boy. He didn't have any compassion at all.

"You probably wonder why I come to visit you, right? Shall I tell you?" The boy paused dramatically before he continued, as if he had received some form of confirmation. "All right, then. Maybe I just thought, now that mother is no longer among the living, you might be a bit lonely, longing for a little entertainment."

Wolfgang noticed his anger boiling up inside. He felt no desire to listen to his son or even see him again. Not since their last encounter, after the death of his wife, when he had bent down very close to his ear to say goodbye and whispered, "Now the old witch is waiting for you in hell. Who would have thought that you'd survive the old hag? Don't let her wait too long!"

He would have loved to yell at him that they didn't have anything more to say to each other and that Tom should leave and never come back. But his useless lips remained silent.

"Do you want to tell me how you're doing, Dad?" Tom asked with faked pity before he theatrically put his hand to his mouth. "Oh, you still can't talk, right?" The hand in front of the mouth disappeared and revealed a big grin. "Pretty shitty, huh? Can you do anything but blink? No? Still not? Shall we do it the same way as last time: You blink once for yes and twice for no when I ask you a question?" Wolfgang quickly blinked twice. He didn't feel like communicating with that asshole he used to call his son. The boy was the biggest disappointment of his life. He had raised a stranger, an emotionally cold monster who had nothing in common with the man he had wanted to raise him to.

"No? Don't be silly, Pop. That's how we do it. Do you understand?" Reluctantly Wolfgang blinked once.
108

Tom wouldn't leave anyway until he had got what he wanted.

"Well, it's all right," Tom nodded contentedly. "Do they take good care of you here?"

A blink.

"I met a really hot nurse in the hallway. Don't you wish you were young again to give her the fuck her brains out?"

The only wish Wolfgang had lately was to die soon. He hated this helpless existence. His mind was still intact, but he had to be fed, washed and diapered like a toddler. Except for the ring finger and the little finger of his right hand, he couldn't move any of his limbs. He had lost his ability to speak. He could still think, but his mouth refused to translate his thoughts into words. He couldn't even ask for a glass of water when he was thirsty. He had been vegetating for three years. An improvement in his condition was no longer to be expected after such a long time. So he blinked twice.

"I finally know what I'll do with the house," Tom continued in a casual chat. "I've made some changes in the last few weeks. You'd be surprised if you could see what I did."

Wolfgang knew that he would never return to this house where he had spent more than half of his life. The second stroke had turned him into a helpless nursing case. Since then Wolfgang expected death every day – that miserable son of a bitch who simply didn't want to come get him.

"Do you remember the basement? You often locked me up down there when I was a child."

Of course Wolfgang could remember. Tom had been a wild boy. So wild that he sometimes had to punish him. He and his wife had always been reluctant towards

109

harsh punishments. They wanted to raise their boy with love and understanding, had always tried to be good parents for him. Wolfgang had only unwillingly raised his hand. But sometimes the boy had done things that you couldn't just let him get away with. How often had the parents of beaten children complained to him, or his overburdened teachers, who couldn't control Tom's behavior any better than he and his Elisabeth?

"I even like to remember it. I always enjoyed it down there. Did you know that? That's why I've extended my cellar a little now. It really turned out great. Well, except for one little thing. Unfortunately I drilled a pipe when I wanted to anchor some hooks in the ceiling. Knocked out the electricity in the whole house. I would call an electrician to repair it, but I don't think that would be so good. He could discover my little hobby room, right? That's why I just bought a generator, so I can produce the little bit of electricity I need myself. Maybe it's even practical. If there's never a light upstairs, it looks even more like nobody is there anymore. I also nailed the windows with laths to complete the impression. I didn't water my mother's flower beds all summer. And do you know what's the worst? I don't even mow the lawn on Saturdays!"

Dull horror crept into Wolfgang. He suspected that he didn't want to know at all what Thomas had in mind with all this effort and what he was doing in his cellar. He had never wanted to admit it, but the boy had a terrifying dark side, something evil deep inside of him.

"Do you remember that I always wanted a dog as a child? You never gave me one, however much I begged for one. Why not?"

Wolfgang thought of how he had caught the boy when he tortured the neighbor's cat. Before that it had

110

been much easier to close one's eyes and blame the death of some pets on an accident or an unintentional mistake. But to buy a dog, no, that wasn't a good idea!

Thomas leaned a little closer to him and stared straight into his eyes as he asked his next question, "It was because of the cat, right?"

A blink.

Satisfied, he now leaned back. "It's nice that we can finally talk honestly with each other. Back then, on that day in the basement, you wouldn't have understood me. Probably you still lack the understanding for me today. But what do you want to do? You can't release the cat again or make me realize with a cigarette stub how impossible my behavior is, can you? Shall I tell you something, father? Nothing is impossible!"

Wolfgang closed his eyes. He didn't want to hear what came next. But he could not close his ears.

"I have a new pet now, Dad. One that I have wished for a long time. Her name is Fida. She's still very young and needs a little training. You'd like Fida, Dad. She's adorable. I am just teaching her to obey her name and to walk on all fours. Maybe next time I'll bring you a picture of her!"

Sheer horror flashed through the thinking and feeling spirit that was stuck in his deaf body, which now showed a reaction after all. A goosebump, caused by naked horror, covered the entire surface of his skin. *My God, what has the boy done?* Wolfgang opened his eyes again, tried to move his lips to articulate himself, but he didn't produce more than an incomprehensibly croaking sound. Thomas replied with a cold barking laugh. Wolfgang's hand began to wander slowly. With his two fingers still able to move, he reached over his belly to his side. He wanted to reach the alarm button, which the

111

nurses always put into his bed easily accessible. The alarm button that Thomas now held up in the air.

"Are you looking for that?" he asked mockingly. "Don't be silly, Pop. You couldn't tell anyone anyway! Besides, I'm here now. I can help you." Thomas put the alarm button a bit outside Wolfgang's reach on the blanket and took a look at an imaginary wristwatch. To confirm this gesture, he tapped on his bare wrist.

"Oops, is it that late already? I should go now. Finally I promised Fida to come home soon. Shall I shake up your pillow first?"

Desperately Wolfgang blinked twice. No, he didn't want Thomas to get any closer to him, and he didn't want to be touched by him.

Tom grinned, "Yes? Wait, I'll make it a little more comfortable for you!" Thomas pulled the pillow from under Wolfgang's head, took it in both hands and shook it slowly in front of his face. Wolfgang closed his eyes. Now it's time, he thought, torn between abysmal fear and longing expectation. So death comes to fetch me! Then he felt the boy lifting him effortlessly with his well-trained arms, as if he were light as a feather. Instead of pressing it firmly on his face, he pushed the pillow under him before gently and carefully bedding Wolfgang on it again.

"See you next time, Dad. Don't worry, I'll visit you again soon!"

Tears gushed out under Wolfgang's closed eyelids, which he only opened again when he heard the room door fall into the lock.

112

# April 17, 2017

Frustrated, Tatjana ends the call and throws the cordless phone onto the coffee table. Silly as it may be, she actually called the time check just to test if the stupid device works. Now she feels stupid. Of course everything is fine with the phone. It's just after ten and Jochen still hasn't called. Slowly she no longer believes that he will call today.

She feels weird in this big empty house. It's not a nice feeling, more like the one she had as a child when she was sent to the basement to get beverages. It was chilly down there and her parents stored there their crates of mineral water, coke, beer and whatever other beverages they had. There was always an indefinable excitement, a creeping fear, about opening the door to the cellar. To a black hole that opened in front of her, in which something unknown evil could lurk. Then her hand found the light switch on the wall and the fear disappeared, along with the darkness.

Now her hand is reaching for the remote control of the television. It's way too silent here. Only the quiet noises of the house interrupt the silence – sometimes a crackle in the wood or the heating. These are noises that she knows and normally assigns automatically, without really registering them, but today they tug at her nerves. They seem threatening and alien, making her wince in horror. Of course, she was often at home alone. During the day, while Laura was at school and Jochen was at work, but rarely at night. And never for such a long time. Otherwise one look at the clock was enough to know how long it would take before the front door opened and her husband came home.

Tatjana tells herself that it's silly to be afraid of every sound now. Irrational and stupid, after all she is at home here and never felt so insecure before. Nevertheless, she is glad when the TV is running and the unnatural silence and the quiet sounds of the house are drowned out. She turns the sound a little louder, then gets up and goes into the kitchen. There she uncorks a bottle of red wine, wastes no time letting it breathe and pours herself a glass. Back on the sofa Tatjana zaps through the channels. There's nothing but crap everywhere. She takes a sip of her wine, keeps zapping. Somewhere on one of the channels she gets stuck on an old film. 'Invasion of the Body Snatchers' – not the lousy remake, but the 1978 version, which she saw for the first time as a child and which still gives her goosebumps today. But after only a few minutes she switches to another channel. This isn't a film she likes to watch alone, without Jochen, whom she normally cuddles up to when the tension rises. Not a film for an evening like this, when the nerves are so tense.

Tatjana has felt lonely for a long time. But now she also feels alone. Abandoned by everyone. She has a hard time dealing with that, wonders how she can stand it if Jochen won't come back to her. At this moment she longs so much to see a familiar face that for the first time she thinks about turning on her computer and looking at her daughter's pictures again. So far it seemed too painful for her, but now there's something comforting about this idea, so she turns off the TV and goes to her office.

She sees Laura laughing on the screen. Tatjana slowly scrolls through the pictures to the newest ones. She stares at one of them for minutes because it looks so much like an intact world, so very normal – and if she imagines that this scene isn't long ago but is rather a current snapshot, then she even loses the feeling of being alone. For a moment, Tatjana gives in to the idea that Laura is sitting in the cinema with her friends where this picture was taken. The film would soon be over and Jochen was on his way to pick up Laura. The front door would open and they would come in laughing, Laura with a half-filled bucket of popcorn in her arms. She would love to exchange her reality for it.

Tatjana wipes her hand over the eyes, in which tears are gathering again, and takes her gaze off Laura's face. Only then she notices a detail in the background that she has completely overlooked so far because she only paid attention to Laura. Behind the small group of laughing girls one can see the bicycle stand next to the entrance of the cinema. Surprised, she registers a bicycle with flame-paint. That thing looks familiar to her. What a coincidence! Tatjana clicks on the next picture. This one seems to have been taken by Laura herself, from another perspective. Kerstin, who probably took the other photo, is now in the picture. This time Tatjana also takes a closer look at the people in the background and discovers a man who doesn't belong to the group, but seems to look directly into the camera.

*Strange*, she thinks, but doesn't consider it important yet. Only a few pictures later does she become suspicious. It shows Laura and Kerstin sitting on a meadow in the park. On the path behind it, a cyclist has stopped exactly at the moment when the picture was taken and seems to be looking at the girls. Tatjana enlarges the shot to make it easier to see the paintwork, but this also makes it blurrier and in the end she's not sure. It could

115

be the same bike she has seen several times before. How strange to discover it in Laura's last pictures. There are more pictures of this day. She also looks through them now. The bicycle is no longer to be seen. But then, about twenty pictures later, it reappears. The same bike in another place, again at the same time as her daughter.

Who is this guy who was always where her daughter was? Thoughtfully Tatjana reaches for her glass of wine. Her gaze is still directed at the screen, which turns out to be a nasty mistake, because she misses the glass, cannot grasp it properly but knocks it over.

"Oh shit!" Tatjana curses as the red wine floods her keyboard and pours into her lap like a torrent. She's still trying to catch the glass, but it's too late. The thin mouth-blown crystal glass breaks, although the carpet softens the impact a little.

She decides for the shortest way, runs into the bathroom, reaches for an old towel, with which she hastily dries the keyboard and the table. Only then does she fetch the vacuum cleaner for the broken pieces. She carefully collects the big ones before she vacuums up the smaller splinters. Then she tries to rub as much liquid from the carpet as possible with the already ruined towel. When she is finished, she stands up sighing. She goes into the kitchen, fetches a packet of salt and thickly sprinkles the stain with it. Only now does she look down on herself.

"Shit, I can throw those pants away," she rants. "This stain can't be washed out again!" She's angry at herself about the fact that her top also got a few splashes, about the now red coloring of the expensive carpet into which the wine immediately seeped, angry at God and the world. Perhaps it is this rage, combined with her soaked clothes and the bicycle finds in Laura's pictures that makes her synapses make a connection, where there seemed to be none before. She recalls the brazenness of the cyclist when he deliberately sprayed her wet, the strange cargo he was carrying on his luggage carrier, when he almost caused an accident with the bus in which she was sitting on the very day she got Laura's pictures.

What if there is a connection and if it was all much more than coincidence, but some kind of broad hint? Tatjana laughs. Apparently I've already had more of the wine than the mess suggests, she thinks mockingly. In the bathroom she gets rid of her wet clothes and puts them in salt. She goes back to the office, turns off the computer and decides to go to bed. She just lies there trying to sleep. But sleep doesn't want to come. Her brain refuses to simply switch off and works at full speed. As silly as the thought seemed to her at first – she can't get rid of it.

# June 20, 2016

Tom was always careful not to be seen when he entered the house, always parked his bike behind it, so it couldn't be seen from the street. He had an eye on who else was hanging around nearby. He'd rather drive around the block one more time instead of going to the house when someone was passing by and could watch him. The laths he had nailed in front of the windows looked old and washed out by the rain showers in spring that caused the wood to swell up. He let the garden run wild. The grass was almost knee-high now. Only Fredi's and the cat's graves he kept free. He didn't know why. Maybe because the sight of them pleased him secretly and the graves were behind the house anyway, where nobody but him could see them. On the first floor he took off one of the planks so that one could look out of the window. From up there the street was clearly visible, as was the footpath leading to the building and along the property.

By now, the house looked as if it had been empty forever. For years, since his father was in the nursing home, nothing had been repaired, the roof seemed dilapidated and here and there a storm had swept down single roof tiles. The unkempt condition of the garden and the windows nailed with slats completed the picture. Who would suspect that the owner himself took care that it looked as run-down and abandoned as possible? When Tom accepted his inheritance and returned to the house of his childhood, he had made up this plan and immediately started to put his evil idea into action. If this opportunity hadn't arisen, it would probably have remained a masturbation fantasy forever, an unfulfilled dream. However, the circumstances played into his hands and he had always done one thing: he recognized a good opportunity and seized it when it presented itself. On the same day he had measured the cellar and in the evening he had written a list of things he needed from the hardware store. He spent several weeks with his preparations. Although he used a pneumatic nailer to attach the laths to the house and the insulation in the basement, it had taken him a long time to barricade the place and make the basement soundproof. But it was worth the effort.

Because he always paid attention to who was roaming the streets, he noticed something interesting a few weeks after he grabbed Fida. Tom found out what was special about Wednesday afternoons. And coincidentally, Laura's birthday this year was on one of those days. Tom regarded this as a first-class opportunity to prove his dominance and to give the girl a very special treatment.

Ever since she was his prisoner, he hadn't let her out of the basement again. Why should he? But his keen powers of observation and his manipulative mind revealed to him the view one had from up there, after he had removed one of the laths, as a new tool with whose help he could break Laura even more. This view would be his very special surprise for Laura.

*** 

Laura couldn't tell if it was day or night outside. She had lost the feeling for time long ago. The day-night-rhythm that applied to the rest of the world was meaningless and non-existent down here. She now measured time in

119

intervals of pain, in detumescent hematomas, in the fading of a shiner, or in the scab falling from one of her wounds.

At first she had been terribly afraid in the dark, afraid of what she couldn't see, the unknown, lurking in the black corners and jumping at her. She no longer had this fear. There was nothing down here except for herself and some harmless objects. She had been happy with the battery-powered light he had brought to her at the very beginning of her captivity. In his light she had found some comfort in reading the borrowed book and the previously hated schoolbooks, and had counted her bruises. She kept the light burning all the time, begging for new batteries as soon as the current ones were low, but in the meantime she rarely used it. It was dark and quiet, only the small flame of the gas heater gave a minimum of light. The resulting dim semi-darkness of the room was enough to give her some orientation. The darkness became her friend, who embraced her like with loving arms. Her horror came with brightness. When it became light, she flinched in fear and trembled at what the light would bring this time.

She never knew what mood Tom was in when he came down to her into the basement. Seventeen steps led him down into her hell and every time she shrugged anxiously at each of his steps she heard coming down to her.

There were rare days when he seemed quite normal, just sitting around with her as if he were a friend coming to visit and talking to her. Told her about himself, talked about movies he had seen, or asked her about her home and childhood. On such days there was also something normal to eat. Sometimes he brought pizza with him. On other days he was in a bad mood, not at all talkative,

120

and then she had to be careful not to annoy him even more.

"Heel, Fida!" was the first thing she heard from him on such days, after he unbuttoned his pants and made himself comfortable in his chair. Then she had to crawl over to him, lick his boots like a dog and then jerk him off, or even worse, satisfy him orally. Most of the time he was contented afterward, threw her something to eat and filled her water bowl before he disappeared again.

The situation was most dicey when he arrived in a noticeably good mood with a dirty grin on his face. This meant that the hours to come would be extremely painful and humiliating, and the food he finally gave her as a reward was actually nothing more than dog food.

The boundaries of shame she once had were radically shifted and she quickly learned that resistance only made things worse. Insubordination gave him—in his opinion—all the more reason to *punish* her. This word had been completely alien to her before her stay in the basement, but by now she knew its meaning only too well. She had learned something new. As she knew by now, even unconditional obedience didn't protect her from violence, but it wasn't quite so brutal when she renounced resistance and pride. To protect herself, she let just happen whatever he'd do to her. But a strong, resilient part of her hadn't yet given up hope or her own identity.

He tried to break her, to train her, took away her freedom and her own name, forced her again and again to be Fida, whose life was not worth more than that of a dog. But as often as he beat and abused her: Inside her she was always Laura. And she had the hope to be found or that he made a mistake that would give her the chance to escape. She clung to this hope like a drowning woman to the last planks of a sunken ship still floating in the water. This gave her strength as she lay in the dark, bent in pain and bleeding, afraid that the light would be turned on again.

Laura flinched when the naked light bulb above her came to life. His cheerful "Happy birthday, my angel," with which he greeted her that day, seemed like a slap in her face. "I have a surprise for you!"

The tone of his voice made it clear to her that none of the more pleasant visits were in store for her. She found the content of his words no less frightening. Could that be? Was it really her birthday today? Has she really been down here for three months? She'd completely lost her sense of time. Furthermore, she was worried by the fact that he had first locked the door from the inside before coming down the stairs. He didn't do that else.

Tom sat in his chair. He held three packs in his hands, a large one and two small ones.

"I brought you something, sweetheart," he grinned at her and waved the presents. As always, his smile scared her. But maybe, for once, she was wrong and today wouldn't be such a bad day – apart from the fact that she was still trapped in this shithole. Hopefully, she thought, there was something in the packages that she could use down here. Maybe a new book or something warm to wear.

What she couldn't have foreseen was the fact that today was the day he would break her and bury all her hopes in powerlessness and helplessness. Because he had planned something very special for today. Tom handed her the first package – the bigger one.

"Come on, open it," he said with a smile. Relaxed, he leaned back in his chair, grinned and scratched his balls. He watched her undo the ribbon he had wrapped

122

around the gift, tearing open the paper and bringing to light a large cardboard box.

"I think you're old enough for that now," he commented on the content, which consisted of a colorfully mixed assortment of make-up and a small make-up mirror. He asked her to try it right away and smilingly watching her clumsy attempts to put on make-up in the dim light. After she was finished she looked at him expectantly and a bit insecurely.

"Come here and let me look at you," he demanded. Laura's insecurity grew as he looked at her long and thoroughly. She looked as if she had fallen into a paint box.

"Yes," he finally nodded patronizingly.

"This looks good!" When a timid smile appeared on her face, he added, "Now you look like a real dirty little hooker!"

Consternation showed on her face. She hated him, even wished him dead and had unspeakable fear of him, yet he was the only person she still had. The only one who could say anything friendly to her – or who even knew she still existed. The thought that something might happen to Tom and that the cellar door would never open again scared her more than his visits. He had made it very clear to her how well he had secured her dungeon and that she would never get out.

"You'll never get out of here without outside help, which I'm sure won't come. Remember that well, in case something happens to me," he had told her a few days after her capture. "Your little assassination attempt with the compass gave me the idea that it would be wise to have some kind of life insurance. Yesterday I went to the notary and decreed that if anything happens to me, the house will be sealed and simply destroyed. Then you're buried alive under tons of rubble, slowly dying of thirst and agony, unless you're lucky enough to be killed by a falling piece of debris. So don't do any more stupid things!"

This idea frightened Laura beyond words. Sometimes she dreamed of being buried alive and always woke from this nightmare, screaming with the feeling of not being able to breathe and suffocating. Laura depended on Tom, her life lay in his hands. Although she hated him and he had put her in this situation, she needed him. His pejorative words were hurtful and drove her to tears. Defiant and angry, she rubbed her face with the back of her hand. Tom waved her nearer to him so that he could reach her shackle while sitting. He rattled with his bunch of keys, grinned broadly and unlocked it. Then he gave his next order, "Come on, undress!" Without contradiction, Laura started to get rid of her clothes.

"Do you miss your parents?" he asked casually as she undressed. Distrustfully she tried to guess why he asked her this question. Fear, distrust and longing were reflected in her face. Eventually she decided on a mute answer and nodded.

"Yes," he said compassionately, "I thought so." After a little pause for effect he asked, "Who do you miss more? Your mother or your father?"

Nothing.

"Tell me," he urged her when she didn't answer.

"Both the same!" she defiantly said. Tom dropped the subject. At least for now.

"Time for your second gift," he proclaimed as she stood naked in front of him, handing it to her with a mock bow. She opened it and found a briefs and a bright red bra in it.

"Come on, put it on," he commanded. To Laura's horror, the bra didn't have whole cups, but almost left her breasts exposed. Nevertheless, she put it on without grumbling. Then she stepped into the panties, which had a zipper in the crotch. She felt terribly uncomfortable with these things. That was almost worse than standing naked in front of him. She would have preferred to cover herself with her hands, but he didn't like that. He would only hit her again for that. With his next remark he made everything even worse.

"Yeah, now you really look like a hooker!"

Laura felt the blood rushing into her face. Then he suddenly changed the topic of conversation again and wanted to know, "What would you do to see your mother again?"

"Anything!" it burst out of Laura. For the first time in months she stood in front of him without shackles, but this question made her feel even more trapped than before. She started to cry. "I'd do anything for that!"

Laura's thoughts and feelings went head over heels when he indicated to her what she had to do and what she had to ask him for in order to make her wish to see her mother come true on the same day. She looked in his face to see if he was kidding her or just making a cruel joke. But he assured her that he was serious. Finally he grabbed her chin with his hand. He forced her to look at him, looked deep into her eyes and said, "I mean it. You can still get out of here today and see your mother. But first you have to ask me for something."

# April 18, 2017

Last night, she thought about it all the time. She can't get it out of her head this morning either. Of course, the guy with the bike is deeply unsympathetic to her, because he behaved more than rude. Maybe he's just an asshole. Exactly what she called him when she first met him. Nevertheless, he could be completely meaningless. The way he transported his gas cans by bike the last time she saw him was also odd, but not necessarily suspicious. There could be plausible reasons for this. Maybe his car had broken down somewhere or he didn't have any and needed the gas to burn foliage in his garden. That would be illegal, but it wouldn't be of any interest to her – and above all it wouldn't make him a felon.

But Tatjana finds it more than strange that he appeared not only once, but several times in Laura's pictures. Maybe he knew Laura, had somehow approached her or had something to do with her disappearance. The police had asked if Laura had friends or acquaintances she hadn't thought of yet. Tatjana hardly believed that this guy was a friend of her daughter, but he could be a spotter of one of the trafficking gangs that the police were after. Or a brothel owner who kidnaps young girls and forces them to do God-knows-what in his establishment. His appearance would fit this picture; he looked muscular and well-trained. This is exactly how she imagined the bouncer of such a place. A musclehead who has everything under control – especially the girls. *Okay*, she thinks, *chances are I just don't like the guy and he just happened to stumble into the picture. But what if not?*

Tatjana starts her computer and stores the images from the memory heart on her PC before taking it off, taking the other half off the table and putting it back together again. She wishes she could do the same with her own heart. She briefly feels a sting because Jochen comes to her mind. Just as quickly she wipes away the thought of him and the accompanying feeling.

She decides to take the heart to the police. Maybe the content is meaningless, maybe not. Let the officers find out. Her head is full enough. She doesn't need any more doubts to drive her crazy and rob her of sleep. *The officers will check the guy out and my head will be quiet again,* is her quite reasonable guiding principle when she enters the police station half an hour later. Actually, the criminal investigation department is responsible for Laura's case, but it's based in the larger district town more than twenty kilometers away, and Jochen has taken the car with him. Therefore she decides to turn to the local police. Best of all to the officer who already knows her case. Tatjana needs a moment to remembers his name. A memory hook: Sounded like liquor. Likar! Yes, that's the name! He can investigate the matter or at least pass the find on to the Criminal Investigation Department. The main thing is that she doesn't worry about it any further.

She asks the lonely sergeant behind the fully glazed reception desk, "Is Mr. Likar in the house?"

"What's it about?" a metal-sounding counter-question comes from the small speaker next to the microphone into which she answers.

"Mr. Likar is familiar with the case of my missing daughter. He was the first official I ever spoke to. Now I found a memory card with pictures taken shortly before she disappeared. Perhaps there is important evidence on it. It might help with the investigation. Will you please see if he is in the house?"

A few minutes go by before the officer comes back and the metal voice asks her to take a seat.

"Police Sergeant Likar is busy with an interrogation. This may take a few minutes. You can wait for him over there."

Tatjana turns in the direction his finger is pointing. An uncomfortable looking iron bench stands a bit behind her on the wall. She takes a seat on it.

*Shit, what am I doing here?* Tatjana asks herself, when she is still sitting on the uncomfortable bench three quarters of an hour later, next to a nervous-looking, unkempt man who is probably also waiting for a police officer in charge. He holds a folded sheet of paper in his hand, which should probably be a subpoena that he doesn't like to comply with. The sour smell of his sweat keeps wafting over to her, although she sits as far away from him as possible. While waiting, her doubts have time to grow immeasurably. *As with the rest of the investigation, nothing will come of this. I can see how little importance is given to my find by the lightning speed with which they react to it,* she thinks discouraged. She is about to stand up and just leave when Likar finally comes down the stairs.

"Mrs. Wenz, we haven't seen each other in ages. Excuse me for letting you wait so long. Unfortunately, there was no other way. My colleague told me that you had found a new clue?" he greeted her friendly and asked her to come with him.

"Maybe, but maybe not. It's your job to find out," she starts her description on the way to his office. Then she tells him how the heart reappeared, what's on it and what she thinks she may have discovered. She also tells him about her repeated encounters with the owner of

128

the bike. She tells Likar everything she remembers in connection with the cyclist. "As I said, I'm not sure. But it certainly can't hurt if you find the man and check if there is a connection. In my opinion, he's a very dubious figure," she concludes.

Likar nods thoughtfully. "I will send the memory stick to my colleagues at the Criminal Investigation Department so that they can analyze the pictures. This may take a few days. If there's anything on it, the colleagues will follow up on it."

"Can't you just put him on the wanted list? So that you find him quickly? The bicycle very conspicuous, so it shouldn't be a big problem."

"It's not that easy, Mrs. Wenz," the Police Sergeant stops her. "First the colleagues have to examine the pictures. Only when they can confirm your suspicion that there is a possible connection with Laura's disappearance can we take such action. We can't just arrest someone because his bike is on a photo and he has splashed you with water. We've already experienced where hasty suspicions can lead in such a case."

This reference to Wacholski's suicide is like a verbal slap in the face for Tatjana, but it has the effect that Likar wanted. Tatjana nods.

"Yes, of course. I hadn't thought of that in the heat of the moment. You're right. Nobody wants to ruin another life by a false suspicion. Least of all me. But you'll ask your colleagues to take care of the matter quickly, please?" she apologizes quickly, but still can't refrain from urging him to hurry on. Then she continues, "Oh, and as for the heart – I'd love to have that back again when your colleagues have finished analyzing the pictures!"

"Yes, sure," says Likar, "we will keep you up to date. And of course you'll get the piece of jewelry back if it's no longer needed as evidence."

*Yeah, fine, this may take some time*, Tatjana thinks.

"But for now, Mrs. Wenz," Likar ushers her out, "you'll have to excuse me, please. I'll take you downstairs."

Tatjana swallows her comment that a stolen handbag or whatever is the next big crime that awaits him can surely wait a moment when it comes to a missing child. Like the first time she had to deal with him, she is completely annoyed that he seems so totally calm, even though she sees an urgent need for action. But what use would it be to mess with him? It could only turn him against her and would certainly not speed up his work. Tatjana reaches for her bag and walks past him through the door, which he impatiently holds open for her. Together they walk down the stairs. The unpleasant smelling man is still sitting there, and he also seems impatient in the meantime, as one can easily tell by his fidgety legs.

At the bottom of the stairs, Likar says goodbye to her and then turns to the man whose stern smell hangs heavily in the air. While she quickly goes outside and takes a deep breath, she notices Likar greeting the guy with very little enthusiasm. This lifts her spirits and also the corners of her mouth. *Serves him right that HE now has to spend his time with the stinker!* This thought cheers her up a little bit.

On her way home she looks out of the bus window, thinks of everything and of nothing at the same time. Above all, she tries not to think of anything. Not of Jochen, not of Laura and certainly not of Wacholski, whom Likar used like a weapon against her to silence her. At least that's how it had seemed to her. As the bus

130

drives past the abandoned premises and the barricaded house, a bicycle that is leaned against the wall catches her eye. Not at the front of the road, but to the side. Tatjana is sitting in the front of the bus again and sees it as they drive towards the house. She notices it because it doesn't look old and rusty, but new. Because it looks like a foreign body in this ramshackle environment, like something that doesn't belong there. And above all because of its striking paintwork.

# June 20, 2016

"I'm serious. You can get out of here today and see your mother. But first you have to ask me for something." Laura's eyes widened in horror when she understood what he was talking about. But the chance for freedom, an end to martyrdom and the reunion with her mother—if Tom kept his promise—was worth the sacrifice, right? What choice did she have? At some point he'd force her anyway to do it. She'd have to bear it one way or the other. But if he kept his word, she only had to endure this one thing so that she could finally return home …

"Fida, I can tell by looking at you that you understood exactly what you have to do for me," he put even more pressure on her. "Did I ever lie to you? Or did I break one of my promises?"

Hesitantly, Laura shook her head. No, so far he had done everything he'd promised her. But most of the time he didn't promise her anything good. From time to time it was a pizza, new batteries or some fruit he brought her the next day. In most cases, however, he promised her things she remembered reluctantly for a long time.

"I promise that you won't forget this little lesson so soon," was one of those promises she would have gladly renounced. But to see her mother again was too tempting, even if it was difficult for her to believe him.

"Fida, you have to make up your mind. Do you want to see your mother again or not? You know what you have to do for it!" he continued.

Yeah, she knew. And although she had sworn never to grant him this triumph—not voluntarily—she would. He had won. Laura got on her knees and crawled over to the mattress. There she lay down, closed her eyes tightly and spread her legs. "Okay, you may do it," she said in a squeaky voice.

"No, Fida. You have to ask me correctly."

Laura swallowed. Why did he demand that of her? Why couldn't he just do it and let her go? She tried again, "Please, sleep with me!"

"Sleep with me," he mimicked her. "Come on, Fida. You sleep at night. You can do better than that!"

It was so humiliating! Nevertheless, she gagged, "I want to get fucked by you."

"See, it works," he said praisingly. "Now with a little more effort, and don't lie there so stiffly! You have to show me that you want it!"

Only when he had her so far that she lay lasciviously in front of him, begging him and invitingly opening the zipper of her panties, did he come to her, kneeled between her wide open thighs and took what she never wanted to give him.

Afterward, it turned out that Tom actually hadn't lied to her. She had just misinterpreted his words. This became clear to her after he made her beg to finally deflower her and she had survived the humiliation and the pain that followed.

"You were a good girl! You've done well," he praised her patronizingly, then withdrew from her with a rude jerk and forced her to lick his limping cock clean, on which some of her blood was sticking. Then he handed her the last package.

"Now all you have to do is unpack your third gift and you're ready to go." Laura also followed this order. With trembling fingers she unwrapped the package. When the gift lay in front of her, she realized that no matter what he intended: to release her was not his plan. He forced her to open her mouth so that he could stuff the gag that had been in the package into her mouth and lash it with the leather strap attached to it. He tied her wrists on her back and then took off her ankle shackle. Around her neck he put a choke collar for dogs, at the end of which he attached a leash. He pulled her behind him, up the stairs to the first floor. There he led her into a room that was empty and dark. Little light fell through the boarded-up windows. There was only one window missing a lath and a bright ray of sunlight came in through the gap. He led her to this window and tied her leash to a hook on the ceiling that he had attached especially for this purpose.

"Enjoy the view!" he said and added with a gloating look at his wristwatch, "Can only be a matter of hours until she shows up!"

Then he leaned very close to her ear and whispered something to her before he went downstairs and just left her there. Laura felt cold, she felt defenseless and at his mercy due to her exposed position. A warm trickle that cooled quickly ran down her thigh.

An unappetizing mixture of sperm and blood that slowly dried on her. After a while, the pain in her arms began. Then her hands that he had tied too tightly at the joints became numb. Eventually the pain in her arms became so severe that she thought she couldn't bear it any longer before she lost all feeling in it. After standing there for a felt eternity, watching passing cars and buses, a slender figure appeared at the end of the road. A pedestrian whom she recognized as her mother the closer she came. Laura was overwhelmed by a wave of longing.

134

She would have loved to squeeze her way through the gap between the slats, spread her arms out and fly freely down to her like a bird. The longing for her mother and the longing for death mixed at that moment. Laura followed her with a teary-veined gaze. She wanted to scream, to call for her mother, but she remained silent. Not only because the gag would have suppressed her screams for help, but because she believed Tom was capable of what he had told her before he had left her here alone. "If you scream, I'll catch her just like you, and kill her! I promise you that!"

From the skylight, she watched her mother as she walked past the house with her shoulders hanging, a pile of posters in her arms, not looking up. At that moment something broke inside of her.

When Tom returned to bring her back to the basement, he brought her one of these posters. He presented it to her with a solemn gesture after he put the ankle shackle back on and cut the tape on her wrists. "Here, you can keep this. As a souvenir."

Laura wanted to reach for it, but her numb arms refused to obey her. The sheet of paper fell to the ground in front of her. All of a sudden the feeling returned to her arms and hands and with it the pain. It was like a thousand needles being drilled into her now hypersensitive fingertips. She cried out in torment. Then she was blinded by a glare of lightning.

# June 20, 2016

Wolfgang's eyes widened in horror as he saw who was entering his room. His sense of time told him that dinner was just around the corner, which is why he had initially expected one of the nurses.

"Hello Dad," the devil started the unwanted conversation. "How was your day? Mine was absolutely great!" Yes, Wolfgang was sure of that by now. If the devil walked on God's ground, then he had taken this form. And this here—this body, trapped in this room—was his hell. The devil visited him regularly, whispered horrible things into his ear and fed his spirit with terrible images that haunted him night after night. Wolfgang knew what Thomas was doing in his cellar. What he did to this poor girl that half the city was desperately looking for. The nurses also talked about it, gossiped about the search operation and speculated what might have happened to little Laura. But much worse were the details revealed to him by the devil.

The most horrible thing was his helplessness. The fact that he couldn't tell anyone and couldn't do anything about it cost Wolfgang a little more of his still intact mind day after day. It drove him to despair. Simple communication, signaling a yes or no with one's eyes, didn't take much. But to communicate like that, the other person had to ask the right questions. These idiots didn't come up with the idea of holding cards with letters in front of his face so that he could spell his thoughts. Or they didn't have the patience or interest. He didn't know the reason why nobody tried to communicate with him in such a way, and he couldn't ask for it. The nurses rather guessed with grandiose talent, and misinterpreted him. Wolfgang watched as the devil took a chair and sat at his bed.

"Today I have achieved the big breakthrough, father," he proclaimed with audible pride in his voice. "Fida has given up. Her resistance, her virginity. Everything innocent and pure that you would have loved about her has disappeared. Now she is my little hooker begging for my cock. Well, what do you think of that, old man?"

He couldn't resist a nasty laugh at this point. Thomas knew Wolfgang well enough to know how terrible and abnormal he had to find his kind of pleasure and how torturous it was for him to know about it. Now he continued, this time attacking him directly, "When will you finally give up your resistance, hm? When do you plan to die, old man?"

Tears came to Wolfgang's eyes. He had long been broken. How much he wished he wouldn't wake up the next morning. But every day he opened his heavy eyelids and blinked reluctantly towards another sunrise. He hadn't been able to sleep well for a long time. Often he was awake hours before the time when something like life slowly came into the old people's home.

"You should have seen it, father. It was so awesome! The little bitch begged me to fuck her properly. Do you want to know how I got her to do it?"

Inside, Wolfgang shook his head violently, which lay completely still on the outside. He blinked his eyelids vehemently. Twice for no. As always, when he didn't like the answer, Thomas simply ignored it. Then he told him about the mother who passed by the house week after week, where this devil in human form held the poor child captive and cruelly abused her. Wolfgang didn't want to imagine how the poor thing stood tied up

137

in the room that had been his conjugal bedroom for several decades. The room in which they had produced this spawn of hell. His attempt not to imagine the girl's suffering failed miserably, as did his attempts to warn the outside world of his son who was different from all the rest of the family.

In contrast to Thomas, Wolfgang was an empathic person. Not only able, but almost incapable not to empathize with others. This characteristic, which in itself was sympathetic, made it infinitely difficult for him to live with his knowledge. Besides, when he could perhaps still exert influence, he had perhaps allowed his son too much, never slammed him and never set him any limits as he should have done. Or had the boy become such a monster because of this one time when he had lost his temper? Wolfgang didn't like to think of this day. He still regretted that he had lost control of himself, still felt ashamed of it and at times felt deep disgust of himself. But what the boy had done had really got to him at that time. With a sharpened stick he had stabbed the neighbor's cat, which he held captive in a tied bag. The animal suffered in agony, bleeding heavily. He remembered how he had locked Thomas in the basement before he went back to the shed to take care of the cat. The animal was so badly injured that it felt cruel not to end its suffering. But going to the vet was out of the question. How could he have explained to him where these injuries came from? So Wolfgang had done what had to be done. He hadn't managed to break the cat's neck or beat it to death. So he filled a tub and pressed the sack under water until he assumed that the cat had been released. What he had done was an act of mercy, yet he was so sick afterward that he threw up. He had then buried the cat in the garden – right next to where they had buried

138

the boy's hamster. Then he got drunk. He still regrets today what he did afterward. Wolfgang had gone down to the cellar and became so angry when he saw the boy that he soon mistreated him just as cruelly as he had done before with the cat and now with this poor girl. The next day, when he was sober again and saw how he had beat up the boy, Wolfgang was ashamed of himself. He apologized to Thomas, even though there was no excuse for what he had done. Together with his son he made a simple wooden cross, that they put on the grave, which they had to pass every day from now on. Wolfgang always had a guilty conscience and hoped that the boy, too, would always have something to think about. Meanwhile, however, he believed that it either didn't matter to Thomas or—even worse—even brought back pleasant memories in him. Obviously the boy had had great fun inflicting pain on the poor animal.

Now Wolfgang wished that someone would come and grant him the same mercy as he did for his cat. But instead Thomas now held something in front of his eyes. Wolfgang violently blinked his tears away, so that he could see better what was to be seen on the Polaroid photo. Although Thomas had described his crimes to him in cruel clarity, Wolfgang stopped breathing for a second. A thin girl in sexy lingerie, for which she was much too young, stared desperately at him. The sight was appalling and Wolfgang's heart beat faster with excitement.

There was a knock on the door – just a moment before it was pushed open full of verve. Thomas hastily stowed the girl's picture in the inside pocket of his jacket.

"Dinner!" called the cheerful voice of a nurse, who then apologized for the disturbance and kindly inquired whether Thomas wanted to feed his father himself.

"Oh no!" he replied. "My father likes it much better when he gets his meal from a pretty young thing like you. I wanted to leave anyway."

A few moments later Thomas had already swapped places with the nurse and left the room, but not without first appreciatively inspecting her white-uniformed butt. Susanne Bauer, who had just completed a voluntary social year, blushed, but acted as if she hadn't noticed the look.

"Well, Mr. Richter, here we go!" she happily encouraged Wolfgang to eat. Then she noticed his tears, put the spoon aside again and wiped them compassionately from his cheeks. "Oh no! Now don't you cry! Your son will surely visit you again soon. And until then I'll take care of you. So there's no reason to be sad!" A little more blushing she added, "He seems nice, your son."

Inside, Wolfgang screamed out loud, struggled for words, tried to correct her erroneous impression. But only a cawing sound, a mixture of sighing and groaning, came from his throat while his useless mouth opened to receive the first spoonful of mush.

# June 20, 2016

At the time when Tom was alleviating his boredom by torturing his defenseless father, Laura made her first and only suicide attempt. The months in captivity had left their traces – inside and out. To this day she had always remained Laura – no matter how badly he mistreated her. But when he made her give up her last resistance, more than just her hymen was torn apart. Laura felt how she was slowly losing herself. As if soon there was only Fida left and Laura was only the name for a memory of a distant life.

After Tom had left the basement, Laura trembled and cried on her latex-covered bed. A small bright spot from the flash of the Polaroid camera was still dancing in front of her eyes. After an eternity, when her crying-fit and the pain in her arms finally subsided, she crawled to the head end and reached for the battery-powered lamp that was trapped between the wall and the mattress. Her trembling hands found the small switch and pressed it. A dim light filled the room.

Laura reached for the poster, which lay not far from her on the floor, and pulled it into the light of the lamp. She gave another pitiful sob when she read her parents' urgent plea help in the search for her and that they had offered a reward of ten thousand euros for a hint that would bring their daughter back to them. At the same time, great hopelessness spread inside her. So much money – and she still hadn't been found. If anyone knew where she was, she would have been saved long ago. Her mother, she now knew, walked right past her prison week after week without even knowing how close she was to her. Tom could just as well keep her on the other side of the world. What he had told her was true: nobody would find her down here!

Laura looked down on herself. She was still carrying the disgusting stuff he had brought her. She felt the pinching of the zipper in her crotch, which felt sore and swollen. Dried blood stuck to her thighs and on her breasts she could see the imprint of Tom's teeth. At the height of his lust he had bitten her. With her trembling hands she loosened the hooks of the bra. As soon as she had got rid of it, she pushed the panties down in disgust. The ankle shackle made it hard to get rid of it completely. So she pulled and tore on it until the thing was off. The pieces remained lying on a sad heap at her feet. She bent down, picked them up, crumpled up the laundry and threw them into the other corner of the room, far away from herself. Then she looked around in the semi-darkness for the things she was otherwise wearing. Her clothes were nowhere to be found. He hadn't left her anything but the stuff that made him horny.

Laura was overwhelmed by her emotions. After today, there was no more defiant pride for her to hold on to. No hope for rescue if she even saw her mother but couldn't be saved. Nothing but pain, shame, despair and darkness. No life she wanted to live. She didn't want to be Fida, but she would rather be dead!

That thought became overpowering. That was the only thing she could do, her only way out. Laura looked around in the dimly lit room. There was nothing she could use to put her thoughts into action. No pills, no knife, no … The make-up mirror! Laura took it and smashed it on the floor. She picked out the biggest shard and moved it carefully over the thin skin on her wrists – then with more pressure, so that the shard cut

142

into the flesh, but too weak to seriously injure her. The fear of the pain held her back. She tried again, but couldn't cut deep enough.

"Shit!" she cried and sniffingly pulled up the snot in her nose. Then she tried to motivate herself: "Come on! Don't be such a damn baby! You're a woman now!" She laughed hysterically. Again she pressed the sharp edge into her skin, tried to get all her courage together and cut deeply into her flesh. Only hesitantly did she dare another cut. Finally she let her trembling hand sink. She couldn't do it. Nevertheless Laura wasn't yet ready to forget this last chance to escape. She had a new idea. Hastily she moved the chair directly under the place where the chain was attached to the ceiling. Then she went back to the mattress, picked up the broken mirror and cut the latex sheet into strips narrow enough to be threaded through the links of the chain. Then she climbed onto the chair, put the chain around her neck, and wove it with the latex strips to a tight noose.

With wobbly legs she stood on the chair. She hoped it wouldn't hurt. She had once read in a book that death by hanging is quick because the neck of the hanged person breaks when they fall. "Just a little crack, then it's over," she encouraged herself once more. She took a deep breath before resolutely kicking the chair away from under her.

When the chair slipped to the side, she dangled in the noose, which dug painfully into her neck, but didn't break it. Cold and tight it cut off her air. Laura was suffocating slowly and painfully. She began to wriggle in panic, knowing all of a sudden that she had made a terrible mistake. She had been wrong! No, she didn't want to die yet! As she slowly ran out of air, her survival instinct awakened and made her fight for her life. But the fidgeting only made things worse. The chain dug deeper into her throat. She clung to the chain above the noose, trying to reduce the pressure on her windpipe. She wheezed, could barely breathe. Using her last strength, she tried to hold herself up with one hand and to use the other hand to loosen the knots that had been tied tightly …

# April 18, 2017

At home Tatjana immediately rushes to the phone, dials Likar's direct number and listens to the ringing until a voice coming from the tape advises her to try again later. She dials again, this time simply the number of the local police station. After a few seconds she reaches the central office and asks if Likar is available. They try, then they apologize and tell her the colleague is probably still in the middle of an interrogation. She asks them to tell him to call her urgently. As quickly as possible. She is sure that the bicycle she saw leaning against the old house belongs to the man she suspects. She thinks that if Likar gets back to her immediately and the police react quickly, then they can find him right there and put him through the wringer.

Tatjana takes the telephone with her to the office, sits down at the computer and looks at Laura's pictures again. Yes, it's the same bike. No doubt about it! What was this guy doing on the dilapidated premises? Minute by minute, her eyes wander to the telephone. Ten minutes pass, then twenty. For the first time in hours, Jochen comes to her mind. He still hasn't called either. Tatjana decides not to wait any longer. She'll call Jochen, tell him about her discovery in the pictures and ask him to call it a day and to go to the old house with her.

"If the police don't react," she thinks out loud, "we just have to confront him ourselves and find out if he had anything to do with Laura or her disappearance." She doesn't want to go alone. The guy was so insolent when he splashed her with water. And he seemed pretty muscular. Surely it would be better to have someone by her side in case she puts him in trouble with her questions. Not that Jochen is a great fighter, but she would feel safer with him at her side.

Tatjana presses the speed dial, a little later she hears the dial tone, and after several rings Jochen answers his cell phone. She doesn't waste any time with long explanations. "Jochen, you have to come here! I looked at Laura's pictures again and found something in them. A suspect. I've already been to the police. Jochen, I know where this man is right now. You must come and we have to …"

"Tatjana, it's not a good moment," he interrupts her. He sounds nervous, "I'm up to my neck in work here and can't just leave. That's not possible. And if you've been to the police anyway, they can take care of it."

"Jochen, I don't think you understand," Tatjana says, contradicting him. He sharply cuts off her word, "No, Tatjana! YOU don't understand! I had asked you to give me a few days to think. You can't just call me and demand …"

"Jochen, will you come back to bed?" Softly, coming from the background, but still clearly understandable, a female voice interrupts his flow of speech.

"Who was that?" asks Tatjana. All of a sudden she has become clairaudient.

"What?" Jochen pretends to be unknowing.

"Jochen, stop taking me for a sucker!" Tatjana now screams into the receiver. "I'm not deaf! In whose bug-ridden bed should you crawl back?"

"Tatjana, listen, you shouldn't find out like that. I wanted to explain it to you in peace when I …," he stammers a little helplessly.

"When what?" Tatjana's voice is about to crack, "EXPLAIN IT TO ME IN PEACE?" She suddenly

146

realizes what those words mean. Jochen has long since found some slut to amuse himself with while she almost loses her mind worrying about their child. A worry with which he leaves her completely alone. A wave of hatred swashes over her, reversing the love and longing that she previously felt and turning it into a sheer rage in a matter of seconds.

"Save your explanations! You're an asshole! A dirty, whoring pig! Everything has been said between us! Don't ever show up here again, hear me? I wish you and your little bitch a nice life!" She doesn't bother to end the conversation by pressing a button. Instead, she throws the phone against the wall with full force. The cheap plastic it's made of shatters and rains in pieces on the floor. Tatjana runs to the bedroom, pulls the clothes that he didn't take with him out of the closet. Soon an untidy heap lies at her feet. Now she storms into the kitchen, opens the cupboards there and rummages through them for sacks of the old clothes collection that could still be lying there somewhere. She finds none, but a box of barbecue lighter and spirit.

"That will do!" she decides, scolding loudly. Angrily she drags Jochen's shirts, suits and ties as well as his casual clothes and underwear down into the living room. Soon a fire blazes in the fireplace, but the feeling of comfort doesn't want to arise. Tatjana sits in front of it and stares into the flames. It hurts that he cheated on her. In all these years she has always trusted him and it had never occurred to her that he could look for another one. She can remember the many evenings in which he came late from work, especially in the last few weeks. The lipstick on his shirt collar, which she discovered after the company's Christmas party last year.

"Don't freak out," he had said to her when she asked him about it. "The boss' secretary was completely drunk and flung her arms around my neck under a mistletoe. I had trouble shaking her off. Something must have stuck to my shirt. That doesn't mean anything at all! You know what such festivities are like!"

The first load of his clothes is almost burned. She opens the glass window of the fireplace to throw in more inflammable material, then quickly closes it again because of the stench of burning cotton and polyester fibers, watching them burn to rubble and ashes.

*Has the affair been going on that long? Was the lipstick from the new girl?* she asks herself now. *Has he been cheating on me for months and I was too blind and stupid to see it?*

Tatjana doesn't know whether she should be angrier on Jochen or herself, because she was so naive and stupid to believe all the excuses he gave her. Looking back, she becomes suspicious and realizes that he probably lied to her more than once to cover up his actual activities.

The dinners with clients on his credit card statement now seemed just as questionable to her as any delay that he blamed on heavy traffic on his way home, or on working overtime. The trust she had in Jochen before is shattered. Now she questions everything that seemed normal and self-evident to her before.

As the fire heats her cheeks, her anger cools slowly. It is replaced by pain and disappointment at the betrayal. After she has repeatedly ignited the fireplace again, she remembers the destroyed telephone and the call from Likar, for which she waited so nervously.

"Shit!" she sighs. "He's probably tried to call me a thousand times!" She stands up awkwardly. Her joints are rusty due to the long unusual sitting posture. Tatjana hurries into her office, picks up the parts of the destroyed apparatus and examines them. There is nothing she can do. The phone is ready for the garbage can.

*Just as fucked up as my marriage and the rest of my life!*, is her frustrated thought about it. She looks for her cell phone, which she rarely uses, finds it in her handbag and calls the police station again. She's told that Likar has already left and she could call him tomorrow. Tatjana suppresses a curse, forces herself to thank him friendly and hangs up again. Helplessness now reigns in her and brings tears to her eyes.

"What shall I do now? Dammit! What can I do?" she asks again and again into the silence of the house. Her helplessness extends to all her problems: To Jochen, to the suspect, who will certainly not be there tomorrow and who will slip through the police's fingers, and also quite simply to the question of what she should do now. Call Jochen again? Look for him? Go alone to find the suspicious man? Or just throw in some logs, stare into the flames and do nothing but maybe open a bottle of wine and try to drown her grief and questions in it? It's still early, just 2 p.m., as a glance at the clock reveals. Normally she wouldn't drink anything alcoholic at that time of day. But at the moment everything seems pointless and desolate to her.

*Why shouldn't I?* A little later she has put her thoughts into action and lies with heavy red wine and a just as heavy mind in front of the fireplace. When the bottle is half empty and Tatjana, who hasn't eaten all day, is quite drunk, her eyes get heavier and heavier. She curls up on the thick carpet and falls asleep.

# June 25, 2016

What Laura had done made Tom think. Not fundamentally. Not in such a way that he suddenly found that he wasn't allowed to keep anyone imprisoned in his cellar, but so far that he thought about the living conditions in the cellar. Okay, vegging out on a mattress, with a bucket to shit and a bowl to eat, that was degrading and he liked that. But it probably led his victim too far to her limits. And basically it pissed him off to always have to empty the stinking bucket and to drag water for washing to the cellar.

That had been enough for him for three months – and for Fida it had to be enough as well. But now that he had thoroughly considered what to do next, he saw the need to improve the conditions in the cellar at least a little. He benefited from his undeclared work on various construction sites. What he needed for the planned remodeling, he could take mostly from the house and buy the rest at the home improvement center. Tom was secretly annoyed that he hadn't had this idea at the beginning. The remodeling cost him several days. First he took care of the chain with the ankle shackle, which had been attached to a hook on the ceiling until then, inaccessible for Fida. Since this had turned out to be a bad idea, he made a hole in the floor, attached the chain there and filled the hole with quick-drying cement. He removed the sink from the bathroom next to the former parent's bedroom, as well as the toilet, and reinstalled both in the basement. His construction was dilettantish, not perfect, and a little leaky, but it was better than the bucket. Now Fida could wash herself down there without him always having to bring water down to her. It was cold, but hey, that was better than nothing, right? With a little patience she could warm up a little bit of it with the gas heater at any time.

Electricity was still a problem. Since he had damaged the power line, the generator really seemed to be the only solution if he wanted to supply the basement with electricity. From above, he drilled a second hole and laid a cable so that he could supply power from the generator not only to the one light bulb on the ceiling, but also to a power strip. The kitchen table went downstairs along with two chairs. He placed a kettle and a camping hotplate on it, as well as a few small pots and a pan. If Fida was good, he could let the generator run, even if he wasn't there, then she could make herself something to eat. He also managed to carry two cupboards downstairs. One for supplies, the other for Fida's things. He filled the supply cabinet with canned food, peas, carrots, canned fruit and a few packs of soup. After a brief consideration, he attached a padlock to the cabinet. She would have to earn some luxury!

Tom got a few LED lights that used very little power and batteries. He placed some shelves on the wall where he placed the books that his mother had left, and in one corner of the room he even placed her armchair in which she had always read. The mattress got a new latex cover and on top of that he draped some pillows and a warm duvet. He could not resist to dampen the good mood a bit and nailed one of the search posters to the wall. When he was finished, he looked around with satisfaction. Much better! She could stand it here, right? A busy weekend lay behind him and he thought the result was something to be proud of.

Tom went up to the parent's bedroom where Fida, tied up since the early morning, waited for him to take her to her new home.

"All right, my pretty girl, let's go! I'm sure you're very excited about what awaits you!" With these words he freed her tied legs and pulled her to her feet. He didn't loosen the shackles around her wrists and also left the blindfold on. He waited a little while until he was sure that her legs were carrying her before he roughly grabbed her by the arm and dragged her with him.

"Mind the step!" he warned her just before they reached the stairs, but still had to grab her hard so she wouldn't fall. She gave a frightened scream, suppressed by the gag, when the first step made her stumble. Insecure, Fida walked down one step at a time, trying to feel her way with her feet.

Arriving in the cellar, Tom first put the ankle cuff on Fida, with which she could now only hang herself lying down, as he mockingly thought. Then he released the shackles on her hands and watched in amusement as she stood there rubbing her aching wrists, but she didn't dare to loosen her gag or blindfold under which thick tears came out. The blood probably returned to her numb arms and gave her needle-like pain. Yet she didn't make a sound. Due to the gas heater it wasn't cold in the room, but she trembled violently. Tom couldn't tell exactly whether it was from fear or excitement. Probably a little of both.

Tom took out his knife and freed Fida from her clothes, so that she stood in front of him in her underwear. He enjoyed her sight for a moment before he stepped behind her, loosened her gag and took it out of her mouth. Fida remained very still, didn't move and didn't make a sound. Now he took off her blindfold and

152

stepped back to observe her reaction. Whatever Fida had expected, it probably wasn't this.

She looked around the room in disbelief.

"Well, how do you like your new home?" Tom asked curiously.

Fida looked down at herself, at her ankle shackle, followed its course to where it was embedded in concrete.

"You're not serious, right?" was her stunned first reaction.

"Of course I am!" Tom grinned. "I know it's still not the Ritz, but it's a place to stay, right? You even have something to read so that you don't get bored. Come on, look around!"

Fida went over to the reading corner that had been set up especially for her and took a book from the shelf. "You want me to read that stuff?" she asked him disgustedly, showing him one of the romantic novels his mother had liked. Tom didn't like her rebellious tone at all. He made a few steps in her direction. Fida surprised him. Fighting, she reacted to his approach, took a swing and threw the book against his head.

"Shit! Are you crazy?" Tom roared and stormed towards her with his fists raised. Fida stepped back, grabbed another book as she backed away, and aimed at him again. She narrowly missed. From the table she grabbed the pot, which also had to serve as a projectile. Then he was with her and taught her lesson with a few targeted punches. A swinging blow into her stomach caused her to collapse breathlessly and crooked in pain.

Tom looked down on her and thought about what punishment he should give her for this insubordination or whether it would be better, perhaps even more pleasurable, to take things slowly. A glance at his wristwatch answered his question. It was almost evening and Tom had set himself the goal of visiting his father today. There hadn't been time for that in the last few days, and although it wasn't solicitude that urged him to visit, he didn't want to postpone it. He had other reasons, today more than ever. Moreover, his pleasure was never neglected during these visits. Even if he didn't touch the old man, Tom had great fun tormenting him with his words and the knowledge he imposed on him.

He softly kicked Fida, who was still crouching on the floor.

"I gotta go out again. In the meantime, you can clean up the mess you've wreaked here. I'll be back in two or three hours. Then we will have a lot of fun together, I promise you!"

# June 25, 2016

Today everything took longer. Wolfgang was awake much too early and stared out of the window. He saw the sun rise and wasn't surprised when he heard his door open shortly afterward. A nurse came into the room, checked the air, look at him and hurried out again.

*Yeah, I'm still alive, you stupid bitch!* he moaned with his eyes after her. *And I didn't shit myself, if that's why you sniffed like a pig looking for truffles. I'll wait with that for Susi to come!*

He didn't like this one here: Beate Fröhlich. Just because he couldn't give an answer, she didn't seem to think it necessary to be polite and respectful with him. She didn't even have a 'good morning' left for him. Her name was a lie.

Wolfgang wasn't in the best of moods that day anyway, but it got even worse as his breakfast was brought by this unfriendly bitch. Moreover, much too late, as he discontentedly noticed. Beate quickly dealt with him, loveless and impatient. She urged him to swallow faster. Wolfgang missed Susanne, the young thing in the social year who usually fed him. Susi was mostly in a good mood – and she talked to him while she gave him food, chatted happily with him and made the meal entertaining. He learned from the bitch's nagging that without even calling, Susi hadn't shown up for duty today. On top of that, two others had called in sick.

"I should have eight hands, not two. And it still wouldn't be enough," Beate let go of her frustration as she stuffed another spoonful into Wolfgang's mouth.

Wolfgang swallowed, but some of the mush came out again.

"Be a good boy and swallow!" With the spoon, Beate picked up what ran out of the corners of his mouth and put it back into his mouth. Then she wrinkled her nose. Yes, she had smelled right. Meanwhile his diaper had to be changed. This discovery and the unpleasant smell made her hurry all of a sudden. As soon as Beate had given him the last spoon and checked that he had swallowed everything, she grabbed the dishes and, leaving the room in a hurry, announced, "I'll send somebody to clean you up right away."

'Right away' proved to be a flexible term. Maybe she had forgotten or the other carers were overworked, but half an hour later nobody had come to put this announcement into action. Wolfgang was very annoyed.

Another twenty minutes, which felt much longer, had to pass before the unfriendly Beate put her wrinkled nose back into the room and cleaned him with her usual impatience and open disapproval.

The delays in the schedule continued throughout the day. So Wolfgang wasn't surprised when Thomas came at dinner time instead of the food. The whole day he hadn't had anything else to do but to be upset and to wait to be hectically handled. None of his days were great, but today was hard to beat in a negative sense. This visit topped off the day.

"So, old man, how are you?" Thomas started the conversation. "Long time no see!"

That was true. Thomas had scarcely been here the last days. Wolfgang looked him from the corner of his eye. His clothes were dusty and dirty, as if he just came from a construction site. Soil stuck to his pants as if he had dug up the garden. His hair also looked dusty. What had the boy been doing?

Thomas didn't let him guess for long, "I did something at the house. It seemed necessary to me." Then he described to him in detail what he had done during the last days. At first Wolfgang listened with relief. It was a blessing in disguise—and he now had an eye for it—that Thomas improved the living conditions in his terrible dungeon. But when he found out the reason and Thomas told him in detail how this poor desperate girl had built herself a gallows, his hair once again stood on end in horror. Thomas was not quite finished with his much too graphic description when he was interrupted. The grumpy nurse was still on duty. For the first time on this day Wolfgang was really happy to see Beate Fröhlich, who brought him dinner at that moment.

"Sorry, we're a little behind today. I have to feed your father now," she addressed Thomas directly while she completely ignored Wolfgang. Perhaps she hoped that Thomas would offer to take over this task. He looked at the nurse with a knowing, mocking grin. One could already tell her unwillingness by these few words. Inwardly Wolfgang boiled with anger and disgust. Anger at Thomas, disgust at what he had done, irrepressible rage at this stupid bitch, who only had her finishing time in mind. And he was angry at himself, at his helplessness and his inability to speak.

"Okay, I'll be off in a second," Thomas announced loudly, then bent very close to Wolfgang's ear and whispered something into it. Within fractions of a second, Wolfgang's anger and desperation increased immeasurably and his adrenaline level rose drastically. Wolfgang's eyes widened in horror as he immediately recognized the meaning of Thomas' words. His desperate gaze wan-

157

dered to Beate, waiting with her tray next to the door. Everything matched like the pieces of a big puzzle, making cruel sense. And then Wolfgang began to scream: "IDA! OT USI! IDA!"

The adrenaline drove his body to absolute peak performance, enabling him to do more than he was otherwise able to. Nevertheless, Wolfgang couldn't articulate more clearly what he desperately wanted to say. "IDA! USI," was all that came from his useless mouth.

"I'm sorry. Sometimes he gets terribly upset when I leave again. He'll calm down soon," Thomas explained to the surprised looking nurse and simply left the room.

"IDA!" Wolfgang srceamed again and again.

Beate hastily put her tray down and bent over Wolfgang. "Well, what's the matter with you? He'll be back! Now calm down!"

"IDA!" he yelled into her face. Then his perception suddenly changed. She seemed to have two heads instead of one. Wolfgang became terribly nauseous. He tried to swallow, but he couldn't. The contents of his stomach gushed out, splashed into the face of the double-headed Beate and ran from his chin over his chest. A stabbing pain in his head followed.

Then everything turned black in front of his eyes and like from far away he could barely hear, "Help! Quickly! Mr. Richter is having another stroke!"

*I'm dying!* was his last surprised thought, full of gratitude and insight, before it was all over.

# April 18, 2017

Totally whacked, Tatjana wakes up hours later from a
terribly confused dream. It's almost dark, just bright
enough to see the silhouette of the furniture and the
wood burnt to white ash in the fireplace. At first Tatjana
thinks she sees pale bones. A pool reminiscent of blood
shimmers dark red, already soaked into the carpet, and
triggers terrible connotations. In her dream there were
pale bones as well. Her nightmare seems to transform
into reality. Tatjana gives a frightened scream. It takes a
second until she interprets the images correctly. She
breathes a sigh of relief.

It's only burnt wood. She must have knocked over
the glass with the rest of her wine in her sleep. Only
wine, no blood. She rubs her eyes, tries to remember
exactly what she dreamed. This old house, where she
saw the suspicious bicycle standing, appeared in it as
well as the road leading along there. In her dream she
wandered endlessly searching through deserted terrain
and passed the house again and again. In search of
Laura, but also with the feeling of threat, as if somebody
was chasing her. In the end she felt like falling into infi-
nite darkness, and during her fall she saw the pale bones
she was rushing towards.

With these dreamlike thoughts and their realistic im-
pressions at awakening, several images merge into one.
As if her mind were a machine, driven by gear wheels
that had been wedged all the time, but are now finally
adjusted and mesh smoothly. Like a gush of ice-cold
brackish water from a puddle, the next thought sends a
shiver down her spine. Just a moment later she rejects it

again as too unbelievable and too absurd, before returning to it again.

She remembers the bicycle that seemed out of place, posters falling to the ground and ruthless driving behavior, she remembers branches of thorny bushes reaching for her in front of the backdrop of a decaying building, she adds hands reaching for Laura, the fall of her dead body into the well, and she sees pale bones. Fragments of memory combine with instinct, logic and her greatest fears create a gruesome image in her mind's eye. Pale bones wrapped in the remains of an often-washed sweatshirt. Bony fingers reaching for her in search of help. They lie covered under rotten boards, shimmering accusingly in the moonlight at night, waiting to be finally found. Hasn't she read somewhere that many murderers are returning to the scene of their crime?

Suddenly she feels an impelling restlessness. Even stronger than at noon today, when she called Jochen. The desire in her to reassure herself and to know what is fear and what is reality is growing. The boundaries between them appear fluent to her at the moment.

Tatjana hardly believes what she's thinking, but what does it matter if she gives in to this presentiment to make sure that it's just a compulsive idea?

"Can't hurt to go for a little walk when you feel like you're about to go crazy, right?" she asks herself and promptly gives herself an answer, "If you're crazy enough to think you can easily put together puzzle pieces that might not even match to form an overall picture and thus be right, then you should definitely go out and get some fresh air. Can't hurt at all!"

Through her little self-talk, she tries to see the fear she feels at the moment in a humorous light. She tells herself that she's not about to follow a strange urge just

160

because she had a bad dream and some confused thoughts afterwards. The inner restlessness becomes too strong, the inactivity unbearable and slowly Tatjana doesn't care if she goes crazy and starts to lose control of herself, or if her fears affect her actions or if she behaves irrationally. She has the gruesome image of her dead child in her mind … Laura's lifeless body lying in the insufficiently covered well next to the abandoned house. In a wet and cold grave, very close to her. Somewhere the crime must have happened and couldn't you hide a corpse there? Had anyone looked there before? Maybe the perpetrator was there at noon today to make sure it was still undiscovered. She won't get that horrible picture out of her mind unless she takes a look.

Tatjana goes into the garage and looks for a flashlight to light into the shaft, then she puts on a jacket and sets off. A short time later she fights her way through the bushes and teeters across the wild meadow next to the old house. The legs of her pants get wet and soak with water, but she doesn't care. After a short search, Tatjana finds the rotten planks lying on the last remains of the brick ring left over of the former well. They are almost completely overgrown by tall grass. With a pounding heart she kneels down beside it, first pushing the grass and then the half-rotten laths to the side. Then she takes a deep breath, prepares for the worst and shines into the blackness. Part of her expected so much to find her girl's body that she was stunned to see only stones and puddles of water at the bottom of the shaft. Much of the tension she feels is suddenly released and she laughs nervously. Tatjana is infinitely relieved that her strong premonition turned out to be untrue. But that part of her that had believed firmly in her gruesome find is shaken because the end of her search has still not been

161

reached. Although her premonition was so strong. She remains sitting for a moment, looks into the depths and tries to collect herself. Then she rises. Now that she's no longer driven by her gruesome suspicion, Tatjana feels exhausted and powerless. Groaning she straightens up. She turns to the house, to the back of which overgrown stone slabs in the ground lead, which probably facilitated the access to the well in former times.

Tatjana follows the barely visible path, because she doesn't want to fight her way through the meadow and the thorny bushes again. The old path is a little easier to walk on than the rest of the wild meadow, but after a few meters it gets lost. She uses her flashlight, but can't find it again. Either the old slabs have been removed or they are so overgrown that they can no longer be seen at all.

Now she is standing in the middle of the premises and has no choice but to fight her way through the undergrowth again. Soon she has reached the edge of the meadow. Only a little bit separates her from the backyard of the house. It is surrounded by bushes, in former times surely well-groomed and knee-high, but in the meantime grown up to the hips. Tatjana squeezes herself through a gap in the bushes, expects to find firm ground behind, but instead her foot sinks into the loose soil.

She shines with her flashlight and sees that she's standing in a flower bed. Or something that used to be a flower bed. Then the beam of her lamp wanders over something that makes her blood freeze in her veins. Goosebumps cover her body and there they are again, the terrible images in her head that forced her to come to this place. Shuddering, Tatjana realizes that it's not a flower garden she stepped into, but a grave. Several

162

wooden crosses adorn the supposed bed. Immediately the fear and the horror are back. A part of her wants to run away, but Tatjana has to find out. She shines on one of the crosses, moves closer and tries to decipher the carved inscription. 'Hamster Fredi' is written there. The next cross has no inscription, but the wood looks old, as if it has been standing here for a long time. While she tries to determine its age, Tatjana wonders why the ground she stepped into is so loose. If the graves were old, shouldn't they be solid? Tatjana shines on her shoes, sees the earthy lumps sticking to them. Is there another tomb? Slowly she turns around. Now lying directly in front of her, she finds another cross. The wood doesn't yet look as weathered as the others'. This fresh grave seems to be bigger and wider than that of Fredi the Hamster and the nameless grave next to it. She automatically has a terrible suspicion. Here, too, something was inscribed.

*Please, don't let it be Laura!* she sends a silent prayer to heaven, while she bends down with her heart beating with fear to better decipher the inscription. A moment later, her laughter cuts up the silence of the night. For the second time that evening, Tatjana feels incredibly relieved. What she found was a cemetery of cuddly toys – presumably the pet cemetery of the former residents. The grave could contain the remains of a dog, both in size and in name. Carved into the wood in unhinged letters, she reads 'Fida'.

# April 18, 2017

Shuddering, Tatjana turns away from the graves and walks the remaining meters, which still separate her from the house. When she reaches the building and walks along its side back to the street, she notices a quiet, barely audible sound coming from inside. Tatjana pauses. What is that? Confused, she stops and listens. Yes, definitely. The sound comes from inside. An engine noise that sounds like a moped with misfires, bumpy and stumbling. Finally it stalls.

That's strange. She had thought the house was completely abandoned. Curious, with reawakened suspicion, she changes her course and slowly walks along the wall to the back of the house. There her eyes widen. Hardly visible from the street and even from the garden, a bicycle is leaned against the wall, hidden from first glance. Perhaps she overlooked it before because she was too distracted by the pet cemetery. It is not an old rusty model with flat tires, but a flame-patterned bicycle whose owner is certainly not far away. Somebody else besides her is hanging around here and Tatjana has a concrete suspicion as to who that might be. In a place where there shouldn't be a human soul. Apparently the man she suspects is still nearby. Only now he has parked his bike less obviously. What is he doing here? Is he in there? Alarmingly the hair on her arms and in her neck stands up and an adrenaline rush runs through her veins as she hears another noise from the house. A loud rattling and then the sound of footsteps on creaking wooden planks that quickly become louder and get closer. Instinctively she retreats into the shade of the stairs, behind the bush that is sprawling next to it, where she barely manages to take cover when the back door opens with an agonizing squeak.

She holds her breath, doesn't dare to look up as footsteps rumble down the stairs and someone walks to the bike on the other side. Her heart is pounding so fast and so loud that she thinks he must hear it. But his activities aren't exactly silent either. She hears him rattling around with something and cursing quietly but angrily. Only when he drives past her does she dare to move her head and look at him through the branches of the bush. From behind she can hardly tell if this is the man she saw in Laura's photos, but it could be him. He wears heavy boots, jeans and a T-shirt, seems well-trained and muscular. Two petrol canisters hang from the side of the luggage carrier. His stature and also his height could be right, as far as she can tell. Then he drives around the corner and disappears from her field of vision.

Only now does she realize that she's still holding her breath. Panting, she gasps for air. The man, the bicycle, her dark suspicion that led her here and the discovery that this house is by no means as abandoned as it seems. All this must be more than pure chance. Although she would normally never enter such strange houses, she finds herself at the back door just a moment later, checking and shaking it. It's not locked. Squeaking and creaking the door swings open and Tatjana can't help it – she goes inside.

She stands in a kitchen that looks filthy and dirty, but which is obviously still in use. A torn pack of cheese lies next to a pack of toast on the sideboard. Next to a chair there is an overflowing ashtray on the floor, on a spot that looks as if there should actually be a table. A bad smell is in the air, coming from a few garbage bags standing in a corner. Disgusted, she wrinkles her nose.

*How can you live like that?* Tatjana wonders whether the man could simply be a bum who has found a dry shelter in this dump, but the contrast to his expensive-looking bicycle and his external appearance, even if only seen from behind, doesn't suit such a picture.

165

Three doors lead out of the kitchen. The one through which she came in from outside and two more that lead deeper into the house. Tatjana opens the first one and stands in a spacious pantry with empty shelves hanging from the walls and a small key dangling from a lonely nail. Only in one shelf there are a few tools, carelessly stored, and in the corner there is a generator, from which two cables lead away, which disappear directly into the wooden floor – in a hole that someone must have drilled especially for this purpose. An open toolbox stands next to it. A pipe leads the generator's exhaust gases into a ventilation flap in the outer wall – the way they once were installed in pantries to ventilate and temper the room.

Tatjana frowns. Obviously she has found the source of the stuttering moped sound. So that's what he needs the gas for. But why does the cable go down instead of, for example, to the kitchen to supply the stove with electricity? Is there a cellar here? And why does anyone bother to produce the electricity for a house with a generator instead of being supplied with it normally via the power lines? She checks and presses the light switch on the wall, but nothing happens. She closes the door again and goes to the next one. She enters a long corridor, from which further doors lead to other rooms and a staircase to the upper floor. It's dark here, only a little light comes in through the kitchen door. Tatjana remembers the flashlight she is still holding in her hand, turns it on and lights up the hallway. The beam seems to be swallowed by the twilight, to get lost in the tube-shaped room, until it finally hits a metallic object that reflects it back to Tatjana with a sparkle. Slowly she approaches. She has found the entrance to the cellar, the room where the cables end. Tatjana is quite sure of that. The door is secured with a massive bolt and a padlock.

Why would anyone lock a basement so securely? With a wildly beating heart she presses her ear to the cold iron of the door. There's something, right? Didn't she just hear a noise?

She needs to know what's behind it. She checks the lock and shakes it, but it is firmly locked and the entrance is closed effectively. Tatjana checks the bolt. It is screwed to the frame on one side and the door on the other. If she could find the right tool in the toolbox at the generator, she could loosen the screws and see what's hidden down there. Tatjana goes back to the chamber next to the kitchen, finds a screwdriver there and is already on her way back to the kitchen when she sees the nail and the small key hanging from it. *Maybe I can spare the trouble. It could fit into the padlock*, she thinks and takes it.

She goes back into the hallway, tries the key first, but it doesn't fit. She's about to start unscrewing the lock when she's suddenly interrupted by the treacherous squeak of the kitchen door.

# April 18, 2017

As he walks up the stairs, Tom hesitates for a split second, wondering why the kitchen door is a little bit open. Actually, he's always very careful when he leaves the house and closes the door properly. But earlier he was in a hurry, wanted to leave anyway only very briefly, because once again the fuel for the generator had run out. Surely he was careless, hadn't closed the door correctly or the wind had pushed it open a bit. The last days were hectic. There was a big rush in the gym at the moment. His courses were fully booked and he had to reject further requests for private lessons. His relentlessness paid off professionally. Tom was merciless – but well known by his clients for the fact that nobody could harden a body as he did. If he accepted more customers, he'd soon have no time at all for his hobby.

*If you pursue forbidden activities day after day, they'll also become a habit at some point*, Tom thinks. He was in a hurry when he first came here this afternoon. His lunch break was almost over, but since he didn't have time the day before either and hadn't see Fida, he wanted to check what was going on. Contrary to his usual habit, he parked on the street and used the front door instead of sneaking in from behind.

*You have to be careful not to let your everyday life cloud your cautious view! Especially with things that become routine*, he thinks. Today at noon, when he parked his bike far too obviously, he didn't care if anyone saw it. He was in a hurry and just wanted to unlock the closet with the supplies for Fida. Before, he was annoyed that he hadn't just left it open the last time. Now he had to use his break for her provisioning. Afterward he was glad that he had been there, but was upset about himself and about carelessness. Sloppiness begins with small things. But there's no room for mistakes here. Neither for his own, nor for the mistakes his little slut makes in the basement.

That little bitch. Meanwhile she seems so submissive and well-behaved and plays her role so convincingly that you could sometimes forget to be cautious with her. But he had noticed Fida's bloody fingertips. Of course, he discovered the spot where she had tried to remove the laths from the wall and to remove the filling. She had actually managed to loosen some of the boards. Fida had already pulled out the insulating material behind them and stuffed it into her duvet cover, presumably hoping that he wouldn't notice the waste from her forbidden work. She loosely fastened the boards in front of it so that they wouldn't be noticed immediately. But her fingertips gave her away. A closer look at the room quickly revealed her misdeed. He slapped her and then chained her to the sink with a pair of handcuffs so she couldn't continue when he left. And it was her own fault that he gave her the gag, too. She should have left the insulation alone! Then he went back to work – with a growling rage in his stomach that made him treat his clients even harder than usual. After his last course he cycled back to the house. This time he had more time and carefully hid his bike behind the house.

He had already repaired most of the damage, stuffed the filling back, nailed the slats in front of it again and was already looking forward to the going-over he'd give the little bitch. Ever since she has been with him, it had never been boring to have his way with her, but if she had done something bad beforehand, something for

169

which she really deserved punishment, then it gave him special pleasure. All the more reason not to treat her too gently. But then the damn electricity went out again, and he had to get new gasoline before he could have his fun with her.

With a shrug Tom decides to forget about the thing with the half-open back door. He goes to the generator, refuels it and starts it. He coughs, because despite his self-made construction, some of the exhaust gas accumulates in the room. Not a clean solution. The device causes him a lot of work over and over again and has left him in the lurch several times exactly when he was having fun. Maybe he should stop being so paranoid and call an electrician to repair the defective line. He quickly discards this idea.

Still coughing, Tom closes the door to the generator-room and goes to the sink in the kitchen to wash the smell of gasoline off his hands. When he's finished, he rubs his hands dry on his pants and then rummages in the pockets for the key. As he walks down the hall, he's so busy finding the right key for the cellar lock that he doesn't notice the narrow crack because one of the other doors is open. A terrified eye glances out, following his path with a fearful, but also curious gaze.

He goes downstairs where Fida waits for him to return. He notes with satisfaction that she follows his orders and assumes a submissive posture as soon as she hears him coming. She kneels with her legs apart. She doesn't look up, keeps her head lowered humbly. Tom takes the gag out of her mouth. When his boots come into her field of vision, she bends over and kisses them, unasked, almost devotedly. The wrist tied to the pipe of the sink makes it difficult for her to bend forward far enough, but she tries hard and makes it.

170

He doesn't know if she's cold or if her trembling comes from the fear she certainly has. She knows that he's pissed at her. As she leans forward, he can see the spot on the back of her head where she plucks her hair. Shaggy tufts protrude from a scabby area from which she can't keep her fingers. He's already observed several times how she scratches, pulls and plucks, lost in thought, as if she doesn't even notice what she's doing. A normal person would be shocked at the sight of this broken, submissive being crouching in front of him.

Fida is all skin and bone. Bruises in all shades, from fresh to almost healed, are evidence of their recent encounters. The fear of today's is clearly written in her face. The most accurate descriptions would be heartrending and pitiable. Tom, however, is alien to pity. He doesn't have a guilty conscience that would keep him awake at night because of what he does to her. On the contrary, he thinks that his Fida has made great progress lately. She is docile and always anxious to please him. She actually comes close to what he would define as the perfect woman. If it weren't for that rebellious remnant that her attempt to escape shows. She wouldn't have been able to get out anyway. But maybe the little bitch could have removed enough of the insulation to call for outside help. He's quite sure he'll drive this rest of disobedience out of her. Maybe not today and not yet tomorrow, but at some point he will control her so completely that she wouldn't even flee if she could.

Tom's thinking about how to make her more submissive. If such a creature wouldn't have to go for a walk all the time and wouldn't make such a mess, then he could give her a little puppy that she loved and he would punish it if she was disobedient. Somehow he likes emotional pressure best.

171

He has effectively averted the danger of her attacking him in a careless moment. Fida knows he'll never bring the key to her ankle shackle to the basement. He always leaves it hanging up in the generator-room, for safety's sake. So she wouldn't hurt him, even if she could. She would be stuck down there and probably starve to death sooner or later. In addition, the stupid bitch actually believes that if anything happens to him, the house would simply be leveled. He has expanded the story of the notary and his testamentary decree to include a friend who is a demolition entrepreneur and who would inherit and demolish the house without even entering it once. He could then sell off the vacated building site. Tom would have decreed everything exactly like that and his friend would have promised to stick to this plan in the case of Tom's death. Tom doesn't even know if such a thing can be arranged, but the fact that she believes him confirms once more: Down in the basement he is God!

At the beginning it was only his dream to own her for himself in order to be able to do what he wanted to do, but in the meantime he imagines that she will become such an obedient good pet that one day he can even take her with him. They can lead a normal life, maybe live in another city and in a good house together. It would be so much better if they didn't always have to hide in this pigsty. But as he has only just noticed again, they are not that far yet. He would have to be able to rely a bit more on Fida and that she wouldn't run away.

"Enough!" With this brief command, he stops her from licking his boots. He unlocks the handcuffs. "Time for another lesson!"

# April 18, 2017

Tatjana stands in the dark strange room which the crack connects with the corridor. The first available place she could retreat into. Just in time before the treacherous squeaking of the door. The situation seems surreal, frightening and absurd at the same time. What is she doing here, in a strange house, on the verge of being caught as a burglar? She feels less like herself, more like a character in a horror film to whom one would like to yell, "Why are you standing there? Run!"

Who is this stranger who is standing here in the dark and barely dares to breathe because of her tension? She almost expects to wake up from a nightmare that seems far too real. Looking for a way out, her gaze glides through the room, but she can't find one. The windows are nailed, the only door leads back into the hallway. She thinks feverishly, looking for a way out of this situation. Panic boils up in her because she can't find one. Fortunately, she is distracted by her anxiety as she hears the generator being started. She listens strained into the hallway. What's he doing? What's he up to? He will certainly go to the cellar. The best thing she can do is just hide in here and keep quiet until he has disappeared downstairs. Then she can sneak out of the house quietly and unnoticed. With her nerves tense to the extreme, she waits.

Then she hears his footsteps coming closer as expected. She watches as he sorts his keys, finds the right one, and opens the lock. She sees him well enough to be sure: Yes, that's the guy in Laura's photos. He's tall, seems more muscular than in the pictures, but without a doubt he's the one.

Nameless horror goes hand in hand with recognition. Her instinct and the way she found him tell her that this man is vicious and dangerous. He surely has skeletons in his closet. What will he do to her if he finds her? Again the image of pale bones finds its way into her consciousness and she shivers. Now she gazes back at him, sees how he opens the cellar door, goes through it and closes it behind him. The fear that came with her discovery is so overwhelming that she doesn't even want to see what he's hiding from the world down there. At least not now and not on her own. The only thing she wants is to get out of here as fast as possible. Later she can tell the police about the basement room – or rather not? Maybe she would get into trouble, because it was actually forbidden and counted as burglary to sneak secretly into a strange house. *I don't have to tell them that I was inside*, she thinks. It's certainly enough to tell them about the bicycle and the man. She will simply say that she recognized him immediately and happened to see him go into the house with a few gas cans. But she won't stay here and take the risk of him catching her here! She'd love to run away immediately, but she's afraid to venture out of her hideout too soon. What if he only stays down for a short time to quickly fetch something and immediately comes back up again? It's better to wait a little longer.

Because her eyes have slowly become accustomed to the twilight, she now perceives more of her environment. Once again she looks around, more attentively this time. She's standing in something that was once a child's room. The bed, of which only the rusty frame is left, a desk in the corner and, above all, the motif wall-

174

paper, which is waved from the wall, suggest this. Apart from that, the room is completely empty. Only the walls tell something about the child who once lived here. Three carved wooden letters, from which the old colored lacquer peels off, reveal the name: Tom. The 'T' has come loose from the wall, hangs upside down, held by a nail, and looks like an inverted satanic cross. Tatjana is not a believing woman, but at this moment she feels the desire to cross herself. Everything in her urges her to finally get out of here. She has been here far too long!

Quietly, anxious to make careful steps so that her heels don't clatter, she turns to the door again, listens into the hallway and opens the narrow crack a little further. After a controlling look at the closed cellar door, she sneaks soft-footed along the corridor back into the kitchen, anxiously pausing as soon as a plank squeaks. She's almost scared to death when the generator starts stuttering and coughs briefly before finding its rhythm again. Her pulse gets faster, but calms down, albeit hesitantly. She has now almost reached the kitchen door that will lead her outside. Tatjana reaches for the handle and gets ready for the door to squeak loudly and to glide through like a breath of wind and disappear into the darkness. Or to run away in case he hears her and comes running up the stairs. She's about to make it. In a few seconds she'll be safe. Carefully she moves the door handle and startles because at the slightest movement the door doesn't squeak very loudly, but sounds tormented, as if it were a suffering creature in great need. The sound pierces her marrow and bone, pumping fresh adrenaline through her veins. Tatjana stops as if rooted to the spot. She realizes that she stopped the movement of the door immediately, but the scream doesn't fade away. Only part of the sound was actually caused by her. It still echoes through the room, quietly, but still shrill and nerve-wracking. Tatjana's hair stands on end, goosebumps, caused by pure horror, cover her whole body. The scream is horrifying; it's the most terrible thing she has ever heard. Worst of all, it clearly comes from a girl. She fears that her imagination could play a trick on her. For this voice, so distorted and muffled, could be hers. Laura! Is that her child she's hearing? Is her daughter here – and alive? After more than a year! Suddenly the scream stops, echoes only in Tatjana's thoughts. It was an illusion, right? Wishful thinking!

Then the screaming starts again. Although Tatjana still has doubts that it's really Laura's voice, her maternal instinct takes over. She lets go of the door handle, the flashlight falls to the floor. She hectically looks around the kitchen. She has to arm herself. Tatjana reaches for the bread knife, which seems far too small and blunt to be useful in an attack. Doubtingly she examines it and drops it again. Instead, she reaches for an empty bottle of beer on the sideboard. She grabs the bottle by the neck and hits it against the worktop, breaking it. Only the neck of the bottle with its sharply serrated, shimmering ends remains in her hand. As the shards fall to the floor, the scream stops. Did he hear her? Tatjana doesn't wait for the sound of his heavy footsteps. She quickly reaches for a second bottle of beer, but no longer takes the time to turn it into a powerful weapon, but dashes off.

If he noticed her, she has to be quick now. Probably her best chance is to catch him before he reaches the top of the stairs. Maybe she can use the difference in height to her advantage. Cold as ice, without really

176

thinking, she gets such thoughts, even though she was never a fighter. Her instinct drives her forward.

Tatjana reaches the cellar door and the next scream sounds. She tears open the door and pushes her hand, holding the broken bottle, forward like a dagger in case he is expecting her, jumps at her and tries to overpower her. But there is no one on the stairs. In front of her only a poorly lit maw opens, leading downwards, straight into the depths of hell, if one interprets the tortured sobbing of the tormented soul biblically, into which the shrill scream now merges.

Without hesitation, she runs down the stairs with her child's name on her lips as an encouraging battle cry. "Laura, don't be afraid! I'm coming!"

Her gaze falls on Tom, whose head suddenly turns in her direction.

"What the hell ...?" he curses with astonishment. Suddenly and unexpectedly Tatjana—a screaming fury—enters his private realm. He lets go of the girl's hair, which he had previously grabbed with an iron grip. With lightning speed he reacts to the surprising situation. With a few big leaps he reaches the stairs, just climbs the first step, when Tatjana smashes the beer bottle with a powerful, swinging blow on his skull. She hits him right at the temple. Tom rolls his eyes and falls to the ground like a wet sack.

Maybe later she will have time to wonder how quick and easy it was to eliminate him, but now, as she hastily climbs over him, she only has eyes for this girl who is anxiously crouching on the floor.

# April 18, 2017

Tatiana's heartbeat seems to have stopped for a moment. In front of her crouches the most vulnerable creature she has ever seen. Immediately she realizes that she's not her daughter. But at this moment, strangely enough, this seems completely meaningless to her. She feels everything she otherwise only feels for her own child. Within a blink of an eye, this girl has all the love and sacrifice that Tatjana has felt exclusively for Laura. Tatjana drops her armament, gets on her knees next to her and takes the girl into her arms, presses her firmly against her. It's not Laura, but she doesn't care. This girl is the embodiment of all the fears that plague her about her own daughter. The incarnate image of her worst fears. And she, Tatjana, is here to save her!

"It's all right! I'm here! Nothing will happen to you anymore," she mumbles again and again in her ear. "It is over. I will not let him do anything to you again!" Tears run down her cheeks, a salty, rousing river. Although it's not Laura, she's overwhelmed by the feeling of holding this child in her arms. Only when the girl whimpers quietly does she realize that she is pressing too hard. Tatjana lets go in shock and moves a little away from her. Now she looks at the child properly for the first time. She's older than Tatjana thought at first glance. Not so much a child but a young woman. The sight is terrible, but at the same time it makes Tatjana unspeakably happy, because she has at least found this one victim. What has this bastard done to her? Tears are still running down her cheeks.

The young woman looks at her in disbelief and cannot understand what is happening. Finally a sobbing, questioning sound breaks out of her before she too bursts into tears and clings to Tatjana like a drowning person on a life belt.

"My girl! I'm here," Tatjana mumbles at the crying woman as her comforting hands caress her head again and again. "Don't worry, I'll get you out of here!"

She's aware of the danger they're still in. Her gaze wanders to the unconscious man at the bottom of the stairs as she tries to calm the young woman. They have to get out of here before the bastard regains consciousness. She gently pushes the young woman away. She reaches under the girl's chin and softly forces her to raise her gaze. The two look each other in the eye. "I promise you I'll get you out of here," Tatjana assures her forcefully and then asks, "What's your name, my girl?"

"Fi…" She hesitates. Then it bursts out of her, "Susanne! My name is Susanne!"

Tatjana notices that she almost said another name at first. "What did she want to say instead of Susanne?" Even before she asks her next question, she has a gloomy foreboding what the answer will be. "You wanted to say something else! What did you want to say when I asked your name?"

"Fida," sobs the girl. A horror, which now has a name, spreads in Tatjana when she thinks of the grave into which she stumbled earlier. But she doesn't allow herself to pursue this thought any further. She has no time for that!

"Well then, Susanne. We gotta go. Now! You have to be very strong. We have to get away from here! Can you stand up?"

179

"I can't walk!" sobs the young woman. Only when Susanne points to it, Tatjana notices the heavy iron ankle shackle, with which the immediate escape is prevented.

"Shit!" Tatjana moans. In a flash, possible alternatives shoot through her head. She can go alone, bring herself to safety and return with the police. But what if the son of a bitch wakes up and kills the girl before she gets back? Everything in her resists leaving Susanne here alone with him.

"Tom has the key," whimpers Susanne with an anxious look to the still motionless body lying there, bleeding heavily from a wound on the temple. An ice-cold shiver runs down Tatjana's spine as she hears this name, which she immediately associates with the child's room. Has this monster lived here so long – like a wolf in sheep's clothing in a supposedly safe environment?

She grabs the broken bottle to arm herself again. It takes all her courage to approach this monster. She saw him put his keys in his pocket earlier before he went into the cellar. She carefully reaches in and pulls out the bunch of keys, keeping her eyes glued to the dirtbag. Ready to ram the dagger of shards into his throat at the slightest movement. But he doesn't move and she slowly withdraws from him.

"Which one is it?" she asks and tries them one by one when Susanne doesn't answer.

Finally Susanne sobs, "He never has the key with him, so that I don't even think about running away." Tatjana frowns. "Where does he have it then? Do you know that?" Susanne bites her lips, tears shoot into her eyes again and she desperately shakes her head. "No, I only know that he keeps it somewhere upstairs in the house."

Tatjana remembers the small key that didn't fit into the padlock on the cellar door. She rummages in the pocket of her pants until she can finally grab it. With her fingers trembling with excitement, she brings him to light. She needs several attempts to insert it into the keyhole of the filigree lock that secures the ankle shackle. She can hardly believe her luck when the lock actually opens.

Once again Tatjana struggles with her tears when she sees the sore, chafed flesh underneath. But there is no time for horror or compassion. A moaning from the stairs and a weak movement that she perceives from the corner of her eye make her aware that they don't have time.

"Come, quick, we have to hurry!" she shouts as she pulls Susanne up and towards the stairs. The monster comes to – only slowly, but it won't be long before Tom has fully regained consciousness. He is in the way, blocking the easy access and the first step of the stairs. When they reach him, Susanne hesitates. The fear of him is written all over her face. At first she doesn't dare to climb over him. Only when Tatjana urges her again, "Quick, we must hurry and be out of here before he comes to!" she summons up all her courage and takes a big step. On weak legs she staggers up the stairs. Tatjana is also about to take a big step over Tom as he moans again. She has just taken the first two steps when his hand grabs her ankle with a firm grip. Tatjana stumbles. She slams her jaw onto one of the steps and a strong pain shoots explosively into her brain. For a second she feels dazed. His hand holds her ankle in a grip of iron. Instinctively she kicks back with her free foot, hitting Tom right in the face. He howls loudly. The sound of his nose breaking is almost inaudible in his scream, but

181

Tatjana can still hear it. His grip around her foot loosens, and as soon as she is free, Tatjana sprints away, climbing the steps on all fours. She can hear that Tom is right on her heels. His breath sound stertorous and wet. It sounds like a blocked drain from which the sewage bubbles back into the sink.

Tatjana's almost reached the top of the stairs. Like a runner at the final sprint she dashes through the door and spins around. If she hurries, she can slam the door, close the loose padlock and lock him up. But she's not fast enough. While she is pressing the door shut, he manages to squeeze his hand between the metal and the frame. Tatjana now throws herself against the door with her whole body. Tom howls in pain, but instead of withdrawing his hand, he moves it forward, pushing all his weight against the door from the inside and squeezing his arm out a little further. With a bleeding hand and despite several broken fingers, he tries to grab her. He is strong, much stronger than her. Tatjana can only lose a tug of war about the door. The moment Tom throws himself against it again from inside, she suddenly lets go. Not meeting the resistance he was expecting causes him to stumble. Instead of opening the door, he kicks it open and falls into the dark hallway that Tatjana now runs along in panic. That gives her a few precious seconds lead. In the kitchen she can barely see the exit door closing again. Susanne has made it! But she can almost feel Tom's breath in her neck. He is much faster than her and catches up quickly. Just a step or two, then he has caught up with her.

It's dark outside, just like in the kitchen. Perhaps there is no one in the street to help them. *Under no circumstances must he get his hands on Laura again*, Tatjana thinks and doesn't realize that Susanne takes the place of the child

182

she is looking for on an emotional level so strongly that she even gives her the name of her beloved daughter. She has lost distance. She won't let him hurt her again. She prefers to sacrifice herself – but not without a fight! Instead of heading for the exit door, she heads straight for the storeroom. Her good memory and sense of orientation show her the way even in the dark. She flees into it. This time she manages to close the door in front of him and her groping hands find a latch, which she closes from the inside. Tom hammers against the door from the outside.

"You stupid bitch!" she hears him gasp. "You're trapped in there!"

She's looking for the toolbox in the dark. Maybe she'll find a carpet knife or something else to defend herself with. She doesn't find the box immediately, hits something on the ground. It falls over and makes a clattering noise. The biting stench of gasoline spreads through the small room. Frightened, she recedes. Tatjana bumps into the generator, stumbles and grabs around looking for support. Her fingers find the necessary resistance and hold on to one of the shelves. There she gropes around and suddenly has something heavy in her hand. The nail gun! When she was in here for the first time, Tatjana saw it lying on the shelf. She presses the trigger, but nothing happens. How does this thing work?

"Will you come out on your own or do you want to play with me for a while?" he asks from outside. It's pitch dark in the chamber. Tatjana remembers the lighter in her trouser pocket. She takes it and lights it, although it smells so penetratingly of gasoline. The fumes irritate her lungs and she coughs. In the glow of fire she inspects the device and finds the safety lever. The oily puddle in which she stands reflects the glow of the fire.

183

As soon as she has found the lever, she extinguishes the flame. She is relieved that the fuel does not ignite immediately.

Meanwhile Tom rages loudly in the kitchen. He tries to understand what just happened.

"How did you get inside, you old cunt? How dare you break into my house, you filthy sow?" he wants to know. "You ruined everything! How did you even find me? Don't think I don't know who you are!"

Tom has recognized her. This is the first halfway tangible evidence, a clue that he actually had something to do with Laura.

"You're trapped in there!" he proclaims triumphantly when she doesn't answer him. "As for me, you can stay in there for hours. When you get out, I'll kill you just like your little daughter!"

The blood literally freezes in Tatjana's veins. He admits it! So easily? He has killed Laura? A thousand thoughts and emotions flood Tatjana. Then the background noise changes. The hammering at the door stops. Instead she now hears the heavy kicks off his boots and the squeaking of the back door. Then Tom's dark voice resounds again, full of triumph and self-confidence.

"Fida! Fiiidaaa!" he calls luringly into the night. "Be a good girl and come back inside! Then I won't hurt your rescuer unnecessarily!"

There's no sound in the nocturnal silence.

"Fida!" he calls again, more strictly this time. "I know that you can hear me. You're naked and injured. You must be hiding in the bushes back there! If you're not a good girl and come back immediately, then you'll force me to hurt that woman terribly! You don't want that, right?"

184

It remains silent.

"Well, come on, Fida. Don't make me come outside and get you!"

Tatjana understands that the time to think about what to do next has passed. With horror she hears his next words of praise, "Good little girl, come back here!" She must not allow him to get the girl back under his control! She resolutely grabs the pneumatic nailer even more tightly. Then she releases the safety lever, fires a first nail behind her for a test, while she is already carefully opening the door. She hears a *Ping!* The sound of metal hitting metal. Tatjana storms into the kitchen. In the door frame, she can see Tom's silhouette, which is darkly visible. Behind her, the puddle of gasoline hisses and bursts into flames, ignited by the spark struck by the first nail hitting the generator. Tatjana doesn't think any longer. As fast as she can, her finger pulls the trigger of the nail gun again and again. Projectiles shimmering in the light of fire fly through the room. The first nails miss their target, but then they hit.

The silhouette howls, turns around and is hit again. Tom freezes in the middle of the motion. The flames flicker upwards, illuminate the room and now she sees where the nail hit. The nail gun has driven one of its projectiles with force through the palm of his already injured hand and nailed it to the wood of the door frame. Tom screams his head off. With the other hand he reaches for the nail and tries to pull it out. He can't make it. Tom howls even louder, but reaches for the nail again. Obviously he doesn't want to give up without a fight – just like her. Tatjana fears that he might succeed in removing the nail this time, so she aims again, courageously pulls the trigger once, twice – and hits him. The first nail staples the helping hand to the already fixed

185

one, the second one digs deep into the muscular flesh of his shoulder. She did what the police failed to do. She has nailed her daughter's murderer. While she lowers her arm with the nail gun, another shot is fired. The next nail goes into his leg, more randomly than purposefully. She shoots another one through his foot. The material of his boots doesn't seem to be as firm as it looks. The leather can't stop the projectile. The nail penetrates far enough to fix it to the ground and elicits another scream from Tom.

The room behind her fills more and more with smoke, breathing becomes increasingly difficult for Tatjana. Although she can't be sure that he won't be able to free himself with a strong jolt, she has to dare. The way back into the hallway and through the house to reach the front door is now blocked by blazing flames. She must try to squeeze past him into the open. Carefully she approaches the door. When she has almost reached Tom, he throws himself backwards and towards Tatjana with all the weight of his body. She hears the nails coming loose from the wood. He hits her hard and tears her to the ground with him. The sound of his breaking bone mixes with the cracking of the burning wood. Outside, Susanne screams as she sees Tom's body burying Tatjana. His leg is twisted in a grotesque angle, the pale bone of his broken shin sticks out of his jeans. The foot is still held to the ground by the nail.

Tatjana panically tries to push Tom away, but he's heavy. He has stopped screaming. Perhaps the shock from the injury is too big and he no longer feels any pain. Tom is not distracted by the pain or the broken leg. He lifts himself with his elbows, shifts his weight to one of them and reaches for Tatjana, who has almost managed to wriggle herself out from under him. With

186

his bloody hand he slips off her thigh before he can grab her. He holds her ankle tight like in a vice. Pure lust for murder is reflected in his eyes as he growls, "I'll kill you for this, you filthy sow!"

The flames flicker in his gaze. The fire has almost reached them, it is almost licking them with its hungry hot tongues. Tatjana realizes that she was standing in the puddle of gasoline earlier and that a single spark jumping over to her would probably be enough to set her ablaze on fire. But instead of panic, she feels ice-cold peace inside herself. Although during the last year she had often imagined what she would do to the kidnapper of her child, she hadn't intended to kill him. The motivation had dropped even further when the girl in the basement hadn't turned out to be Laura. Tatjana only wanted to put him out of action, save his prisoners, slip past him into freedom and leave it to the justice system to give him his just punishment. But although he has clearly lost the fight, he still doesn't give up. Instead, he holds her firmly and tries to master the situation.

*Not with me!* Tatjana sees red. She reaches for the nail gun that is lying on the floor a bit away from her. One last time she lifts the device, places it directly on his forehead and pulls the trigger.

A hysterical scream escapes her throat as his grip around her ankle becomes powerless. A disbelieving expression scurries over Tom's face. Tatjana pulls the trigger again, again and again. She shoots one nail after the other into his sick skull and stops only when he lies completely motionless. Disgusted and shocked by what she has just done, she throws the nail gun aside. Tom's grip is now limp and lifeless. Slowly Tatjana moves away from him. She feels weak, breathing is difficult for her.

Coughing, she struggles for air. She has already inhaled so much smoke that it makes her dizzy.

With her last strength she leaves Tom's dead body behind her and crawls to the door. She has almost reached it when her body surrenders. Too much carbon monoxide displaces the oxygen in her blood. Her arms tremble, break away under her, as do her legs. Tatjana loses consciousness.

Moments later she regains consciousness and feels herself being pulled over the ground. Cool but still burnt smelling air fills her nose. Every single step of the back stairs digs painfully into her back as Susanne pulls her down and away from the burning house inch by inch. Tatjana opens her eyes. She is still dizzy, her gaze is blurred, but she looks gratefully at Susanne. This brave girl has ventured back into the lion's den to save her! Quietly, far away, she hears the sirens of the emergency vehicles. The fire was noticed. Tatjana laboriously straightens up. She trembles and embraces Susanne. Her arms are still weak. The young woman clings tightly to her. Together they watch as the monster's cave and monster itself burn to rubble as the emergency vehicles approach.

# June 20, 2017

She hurriedly crosses the street and rushes along the sidewalk with her head bowed, through the large wrought-iron gate. Every week she goes this route. Her arms are even heavier today than usual. Tatjana has plundered her garden and picked a particularly large bouquet of summer flowers. It's quite a way into the new and far back part of the cemetery. After about ten minutes it bends into a row with graves that still look fresh. In front of a grave, which is adorned by a finely carved gravestone, she kneels down and puts the flowers next to her. First she removes the bouquet from last week, throws it into the compost container at the end of the path and fills the vase with fresh water. Then she puts the vase back on the grave and drapes the flowers she has brought with her into it, before she strokes her hand over the embedded plate on which Laura's name is written.

Tears shimmer in her eyes, but that's okay. Of course it hurts to come here. Nevertheless Tatjana finds peace in this place. Her life will never be the same again. It was different when Laura was still alive and Jochen was still at her side. Probably the pain will never stop. Tatjana doesn't believe that time can heal all wounds. But it is easier for her to deal with it since she knows what happened to her daughter and since Laura found her last rest here. She now has a place she can go to when she's sad or feels the need to be close to Laura. Tatjana often comes here. At least once a week. She allows herself to mourn, but no longer to sink into her grief as if she were a non-swimmer in a sea of tears.

Gradually she begins to see the positive sides of life again. Jochen is finally history. Tatjana has a home with wonderful as well as painful memories. She now has certainty and can finally sleep peacefully again. And she doesn't feel completely alone either. Sure, she has lost much more than she can cope with. But she has also gained something.

Tatjana hears slight footsteps coming along the path leading to the grave. She doesn't have to look up to know who is kneeling next to her and silently pushing her hand into hers.

"I'm glad you came," says Tatjana.

The young geriatric nurse nods silently and also puts some flowers on Laura's grave. Tatjana knows that Susanne feels great gratitude for not lying there herself. Although it's her daughter who lies buried here and Tatjana would give anything if only someone else could take this place, she doesn't blame her for this feeling. She has taken the serious young woman, whose life she has saved, deep into her heart.

"It's Laura's birthday. I knew I'd find you here," says Susanne. "Shall we stay with her for a while and then go have some coffee?"

Tatjana turns her head. She knows that the young woman still doesn't like to leave the house and suffers from severe anxiety and panic attacks. Even the spot on the back of her head where she pulls her hair out doesn't want to heal. This habit is hard for her to get rid of. Susanne wears a cap to hide the bald spot. Nevertheless, she has come here so that Tatjana isn't alone on this particularly hard day. It doesn't have to be said. Tatjana smiles at Susanne, nods gratefully and says, "A cup of coffee would be good. And maybe even a piece of cake!"

# Epilog

At this point I'd like to thank all those who accompanied me on my dark journey. To my readers who shared the thrill and who hoped and trembled with my characters, but also to those who made this book possible in the first place. First and foremost I thank my children, without whom I could only half as well understand the fears of all parents.

I remember an incident when my children were young. Next to our garden was a small stream. One afternoon I came outside and noticed an old man, visibly at a loss, standing beside the entrance to the canal that led the stream under the adjacent street. When I asked him if I could help him, the old man replied that he didn't know what to do. Children had been playing here, probably they'd been crawling into the canal. At least he had heard their laughter coming out of the pipe, but then their cries for help – finally only silence. Immediately I panicked, my daughters were nowhere to be seen. So I ran into the garage, got a flashlight and crawled into this damn pipe. Everywhere there were cobwebs and countless of these disgusting beasts were sitting on the ceiling. Under normal circumstances nothing and nobody would have made me venture in there. I would even call myself a little arachnophobic. But I was driven by fear for my loved ones. So I crawled through the tunnel of horror on all fours and with a wildly beating heart, where eight-legged beasts lurked and above which there was traffic – ready to do absolutely ANYTHING to save my little ones.

Only when I could see the light at the end of the tunnel again (and the giggling teenagers who had been playing a joke the old man) it occurred to me that my children had gone for a walk with the neighbor and her dog and couldn't be in danger of their lives at all. Since then I have known it: The unspeakable fear that banishes any rational thought, and now I know how strong my maternal instinct is when (apparently) it matters. Without my children I would have probably never been able to write a book like 'FIDA', so my biggest thanks go to them.

I would also like to thank the fantastic team with whom I can work at REDRUM.